CHAMBERS

Bomb scare -Flight 147

LARGE PRINT

BOMB SCARE — FLIGHT 147

Smog delayed Flight 147, and so prevented a bomb exploding in mid-air. Walter Keane was one of those rescued, but he found that during the crisis he had been robbed of his jewel-bag. Mark Preston was hired to locate the missing gems without involving the police. With the terrorists becoming cornered by the FBI, and the suspects for the theft including even Preston's secretary, he had his hands full. When a murder was committed, he knew the stake had grown.

PETER CHAMBERS

BOMB SCARE — FLIGHT 147

Complete and Unabridged

LINFORD
Leicester

First published in Great Britain in 1984

First Linford Edition
published 1997

British Library CIP Data

Chambers, Peter, *1924* –
　　Bomb scare — Flight 147.—Large print ed.—
　　Linford mystery library
　　1. English fiction—20th century
　　2. Large type books
　　I. Title
　　823.9'14 [F]

　　ISBN 0–7089–5021–3

Published by
F. A. Thorpe (Publishing) Ltd.
Anstey, Leicestershire

Set by Words & Graphics Ltd.
Anstey, Leicestershire
Printed and bound in Great Britain by
T. J. Press (Padstow) Ltd., Padstow, Cornwall

This book is printed on acid-free paper

1

I WENT home early that afternoon. It was a Wednesday, and Florence Digby had taken a few days off to visit with her sister in Boston, so she would be missing for the next two days. Her intention was to return late on Sunday, and report for work Monday morning, and she'd gone off in high spirits just before one o'clock. After she'd gone, leaving me careful instructions about how to conduct the office in her absence, I took what you might describe as an extended lunch-hour, and didn't get back until around three-thirty. The place was very empty without her, everything neat as a new pin, and I wondered gloomily how it would look the next day when her so-called replacement arrived from the agency. Replacement, indeed. You don't simply replace somebody like Florence, not just by picking up a telephone. I didn't quite see what the newcomer was going to do anyway, aside from taking calls. She was not to meddle with La Digby's filing system for one thing, and that point had been rammed home ad nauseam. Furthermore, our latest capital investment, the word-processor, was strictly off-limits. This was her pride and joy, and like it said in the brochure, 'the last word in personal computerised creativity', whatever the hell that was supposed to mean. The way it stacked up, I was going to be stuck with an agency fee of sixty dollars per, for the doubtful privilege of watching some stranger painting her nails, and telling me Mr. So-and-so was on the line. It seemed to me that family people should stick closer together. If Florence insisted on having relatives, such as this sister, she ought to keep them closer to hand, and not allow them to go wandering off to foreign parts like Boston, Mass.

I alternated between staring out of the window, and re-reading the sport pages for the fourth time, and finally gave up around four-thirty, locking the office carefully behind me. When I got back to Parkside Towers, I put all the gloomy thoughts out of my mind, and began to plan the evening ahead. I was the proud possessor of two tickets for an Oscar Peterson concert, and I was going to have to make up my mind about who to take with me. On the one hand, it was going to have to be someone who would appreciate the great man, and that part was easy enough. On the other hand, I had to bear in mind that the concert would be over at ten o'clock, which left the rest of the night to be considered, and that called for careful consideration. From the very long list of Peterson admirers, I had to extract the name of one or two Preston admirers, who weren't so easy to come by.

Finally I picked up the telephone and began the hunt. My first choice answered on the second ring, and seemed to be glad to hear from me. After a few pleasant exchanges I said casually,

"By the way, there's an Oscar Peterson show tonight — "

"Don't I know it?" she interrupted enthusiastically. "We have good seats, right up near the front."

That 'we' told me there was no point in pursuing the conversation. I said I was sure we'd all enjoy it, and hung up. The second call was even less productive, because I found myself talking to an answering machine. Making myself more comfortable in the chair, I pushed more buttons, and settled back to the honeyed tones I would soon be hearing. She was delighted to hear my voice, and actually beat me to the punchline. It seemed she'd already been in two minds about whether to call me that very afternoon to see whether I had the evening free. On hearing this good news, I preened myself and patted knowingly at the two pink tickets resting on the telephone table. Was she due for a surprise. Well, no. As it turned out, she wasn't. The reason she'd been going to call was to invite me to her engagement party that night, so that I could meet this simply divine man, who was from out of town, and didn't know many people. I said I'd try to drop by later, wished her and the s.d.m. a long and happy life, and hung up with increasing gloom. The world is full of women who are a pushover for my particular brand of rugged manly good looks, but the difficulty is in finding out just who and where they are.

I crawled under the shower to ponder over this, and as soon as I was thoroughly soaked, and beginning to enjoy it, the telephone rang. Patting quickly here and there, I wrapped a towel around my middle and went to answer it.

"Preston." I announced.

"Oh Mr. Preston, I'm in terrible trouble."

The voice was close to tears, but I could swear it was Florence Digby's, if I hadn't known she was up in the sky, and hundreds of miles east.

"Who is this?" I queried.

"It's Florence Digby," she replied, half sobbing. "I'm in prison, Mr. Preston. You'll have to come and get me out."

Prison? What was she babbling about? Keeping my voice as soothing as I could contrive, I said.

"Now calm down Florence, and tell me exactly where you are, and what's going on."

She seemed to pull herself together in the face of these clear instructions.

"I'm at the Fourteenth Street Precinct House," she replied finally, "and they're trying to say I blew up an airplane or something. It's like a nightmare, Mr. Preston. You must come down here and explain to these people who I am."

Blowing up airplanes was a little out of La Digby's normal range of activities. Somebody must have pulled the boner of all time. Still, that was no help to her. What she needed was out, and fast.

"Now, you're to stop worrying," I instructed finally, "I'll have you out of there in no time. Fourteenth Street, right? I'm practically on my way."

It was getting on for six o'clock, and I hoped Murray Klein would still be in his office. He was a great one for working all hours, and I called him at once. Some dame at the other end tried to give me an argument, but I told her I needed her boss, and fast.

He came on the line, sounding annoyed at the interruption.

"Preston? This had better be good, because I'm in the middle of — "

"Murray, I don't give a damn what you're in the middle of," I cut in rudely. "Florence Digby is locked up down at the Fourteenth Precinct, and we have to get her out of there. Can you meet me with a habeas corpus in thirty minutes?"

7

There was a distinct pause, while he took it in.

"I do have this right don't I? We're talking about your Miss Digby, the lady who works in your office?"

"The very same," I confirmed, "and I'm going to make somebody very sorry about this, so just cut out the jabber, and let's — "

"Whoa," he protested. "Hold on, just one tiny second, will you? What did the lady do?"

"Do? She didn't do a damned thing," I snapped. "It's all a stupid mistake."

"I'll re-phrase the question," he replied calmly. "What is it that someone imagines she did?"

"Something about blowing up an airplane," I told him irritably. "Now do you see how ridiculous it is? Let's just get on, and do what we have to do."

"H'm," and he was sounding doubtful. "Might not be quite as straightforward as you think. When it comes to airplanes, everybody gets in on it. The Federals, the State people, the

Aviation Bureau, just about anybody with a badge. We might find this a little tricky. Don't you have any more details at all?"

"Nope. And I don't need any. The whole thing is crazy, and that lady is coming out of there, if I have to blow up the stationhouse."

"I do hope that won't be necessary. If it should be, you'll make sure I'm well clear first?"

"Then you are coming?" I demanded.

"Wouldn't miss it for the world," he assured me. "I know your Miss Digby, and I have to find out just what kind of klutz would try pinning anything like that on her."

I felt easier in my mind already. Murray Klein is a very tough and able lawyer, and it was clear from the way he spoke that he shared my opinion about whoever put the arm on Florence. After we hung up, I hurried around getting dressed, taking care to select my most conservative clothes.

At six-thirty I parked outside the

precinct house, and walked over to wait outside for Klein. The usual parade of people went up and down the stone steps, while I stood there smoking an Old Favorite, and consulting my watch every ten seconds. Finally, I saw my man, emerging from a dark blue sedan, which he locked with great care before coming across to join me.

Murray Klein is not a tall man, probably not above five six, and he has a spare wiry frame which he carries like the athlete he used to be. He's around thirty three or so, and has a reputation as a trial lawyer the envy of many people twenty years his senior. The face is sharp-featured, with a pointed jaw, and an aggressive nose. His eyes are surprisingly mild as a rule, but they can sharpen up like flints on occasion. He smiled as he approached, hand held out, and winked at me.

"Have you calmed down yet?" he queried. "Or are you still going to dynamite the joint?"

I shook my head, pumping his hand.

"No need, now that you're here. I'm sure you can cause a bigger explosion in there than any home-made bomb."

His face became serious for a moment.

"Well, we'd better not count our chickens, not right away. Let's get inside and find out what these lunatics are up to."

The station sergeant was new to me, but the expression was familiar. There was the same calm, dispassionate, uninvolved look on his face, which carried over into his tone.

"What can I do for you?"

I was about to speak when Klein put a hand on my arm.

"Good evening sergeant, I am Murray Klein, Attorney at Law. Here is my card. You appear to be holding a client of mine, a Miss Florence Digby. I should like to see the officer in charge of the case."

The sergeant's face was expressionless as he took the white card, and stared at it.

"What was that name again?" he demanded.

"Digby. Florence Digby."

"Just a minute."

The man behind the desk ran his forefinger down the register in front of him, leafed back and scrutinised it.

"Nobody here by that name," he pronounced. "Are you people sure you have the right place?"

Klein looked at me questioningly.

"Absolutely," I confirmed, and attempting to keep irritability from my voice. "She was quite clear on the telephone, and she does not make mistakes. I ought to know. She's worked for me a long time. It's something to do with somebody blowing up an airplane."

Up until then the officer's face had merely been devoid of expression. Now it was glacial.

"Oh. That one." Picking up a telephone he dialled two numbers and said "There's two men out here about that bomb woman. One of 'ems a lawyer. Right."

Replacing the phone, he pointed to the low wooden swing barrier which led inside.

"Go straight through through and take the fourth door on the left. Room 12."

Then he bent his head, as if he'd forgotten us. Klein led the way, marching between the desks of the open office. Police officers of both sexes were busy typing up reports, taking statements, conferring with each other in low tones. The impression was one of ordered chaos, conducted in an atmosphere of cigar smoke, stale coffee and sweat. At the far end of the room was a door which led to the inner offices. We went through, found Room 12, and rapped on it, opening it at the same time.

The place was bare of any office trappings. There was a scarred wooden table, with five or six plastic chairs scattered around it. Facing the door, a man sat watching our entrance. He was alone. I didn't like that, and I didn't like him.

Fair hair was clipped close to his head, and his face was almost square. Green eyes stared out coldly from unfriendly features. When he spoke, the thin lips did little more than crack open, just sufficiently for the words to get out.

"Come in," he invited. "Are you the men who were asking about the Digby woman? Which one is the lawyer?"

Until that moment, I'd merely disliked him, but the contemptuous way he referred to Florence Digby brought me almost to the boil. Beside me, Murray Klein must have sensed my reaction, because he jumped in quickly.

"I am Miss Digby's attorney," he replied easily. "The name is Klein, Murray Klein. This gentleman is her employer, Mr. Mark Preston."

Our genial host scribbled our names down on a white pad, which lay on the table in front of him.

"Tell me something, do you only represent this woman, or are you acting as attorney for anybody from the O.P.A?"

I looked at Klein, and he looked at me, each as puzzled as the other. The O.P.A?

"What's the O.P.A?" I queried.

"And whatever it is," added Klein, "I've never heard of it. I'm here to represent Miss Digby, and I wish to see my client, please. Now."

The words were quiet, but there was no mistaking the authority in his demand. The expression on the seated man's face remained impassive.

"We'll see about that later," he clipped. "Meantime, I suggest you both sit down, while we clear up a few points."

We took the chairs furthest away from him. Unable to keep quiet any longer, I said.

"And who might you be?"

The green eyes flashed over at me briefly.

"I am Agent Witchley. I am to take it then, that you both deny any connection with the O.P.A?"

Agent. That meant he wasn't a policeman at all. He was the local man for the Federal Bureau of Investigation. I remembered what Murray had said on the telephone, about all kinds of people getting involved. At the time, I hadn't taken him very seriously, but the presence of Agent Witchley changed my opinion fast. It also changed my attitude. Those federals can do what they like. They can lock a man up if they don't like his moustache. If I was going to get Florence out of this place, I'd better start by putting a rein on my tongue.

"Look," I said reasonably, "I never heard of this whatsit, this O.P.A. And what does it have to do with Florence? With Miss Digby, that is?"

He listened calmly, then pointed at my companion.

"You haven't answered me, Mr. Klein?"

16

"Oh yes I have," corrected Murray. "I answered you the first time. But I'll answer you again. I haven't the faintest idea what you're talking about."

The eyes flicked back to me.

"If you are this woman's employer, perhaps you could explain where she was this afternoon? I presume you work in the afternoon."

"She took time off," I told him, keeping my voice even. "She was on her way to Boston, where she has a sister. I wasn't expecting her back in the office until Monday."

He nodded then, staring down at his white pad.

"That would seem to confirm what she claims. It also agrees with the passenger list from Trans-Continental. A Miss F. Digby had booked onto Flight 147 for Boston and parts east, time of departure 16.00 hours. At 15.15, she telephoned the departure desk to say she was cancelling. Did you know that Mr. Preston?"

No I hadn't known that, and my face

must have said so.

"It's the first time I've heard that cancelling a flight reservation constitutes a federal offence," contributed Klein. "Perhaps you would be good enough to elaborate on that, Agent Witchley."

The federal man rested thick arms on the table, watching each of us in turn as he next spoke.

"Flight 147, as I said just now, was due to take off at 16.00. At 16.15, someone telephoned the airport to say there was a bomb aboard the aircraft, timed to explode at 16.30 hours. The caller said this was a statement, to bring nationwide attention to an organisation called the Oppressed Peoples of America. The O.P.A."

Holy mackerel. Then, if Florence hadn't cancelled, she'd have been blown up with the rest of them.

"Phew," I breathed, "then she's lucky she's alive."

"Very," he replied laconically. "Unless she happened to know before-hand about the bomb. There were forty seven people on that flight. She was the only one who cancelled. Odd, wouldn't you say?"

"No, I wouldn't," I told him, getting steamed up again, "I'd say she was damned lucky, and somebody up there must be looking after her. Otherwise, she would have gone to glory with the rest, and — "

"Mark," cut in Murray sharply, "just take it easy for a moment, and let me handle this. No point in hiring a lawyer if you don't allow him to earn his fee. Agent Witchley has his work to do. It's perfectly natural that he should be very interested to know why Miss Digby managed to escape with her life. Don't forget, we're talking about forty six people who are dead. This is a large-scale disaster we're dealing with here. A few hurt feelings one way or the other really don't matter a damn." Then he gave his attention to the listening Witchley. "Now that we understand what happened, Mr.

Witchley, we are naturally anxious to do all we can to co-operate. Believe me, you are barking up the wrong tree by trying to connect this disaster with Miss Digby. When you've had a little more time to check into the lady's background, you will soon realise that it is quite impossible for her to have had anything to do with this terrible business. What reason did she give for the cancellation, by the way? You haven't told us that."

He was quite right, of course, and even I could see the sense of what he was saying. A few hours of jail-time was scarcely to be compared with being exploded in mid-air.

Witchley listened to what he had to say, then seemed to relax a little.

"Matter of fact," he said, and his tone, if not exactly conciliatory, at least seemed to be coming from a human being, "things are not so bad as they could have been. As these O.P.A. people expected them to be. They knew when they made that call, there was no time to locate that device, or bring the aircraft down safely. But they had a little bad luck. There was fog out at the airport, just enough to delay a few departures. Flight 147 chanced to be one of them. The fifteen minute warning gave us ample time to get the passengers and crew unloaded. Nobody was killed at all, not even scratched. Oh, correction. One man hurt his arm coming off the escape chute."

Well, that was certainly good news for a lot of people. I hadn't known any of them, but I was glad for them just the same.

"That is splendid news," Murray proclaimed. "What about the airplane itself? Did the thing explode, or what?"

Agent Witchley paused, as though considering whether to answer or not. It came down heads.

"No," he replied. "Matter of fact, the security people found it very quickly. It was a crude attempt indeed, and it wouldn't have gone off, in any case. You see, what they did, they made up a bomb with a few sticks of dynamite and, an alarm clock. Then the whole thing was encased in an aerofoil-shaped cover. At least they knew that much, or it would have simply blown off, in no time. Contents-wise, it was just about the most rudimentary kind of device there is."

"But very effective, surely?" queried Murray. "I mean, I don't know the first thing about explosives, but this is the kind of thing one is always reading about in the papers. They may be simple, but they seem to work."

"On the ground, yes. Unfortunately, what you say is true. And almost any idiot can put one together. But Flight 147 would have been thirty thousand feet in the air at 16.30 hours. The device was stuck to the underside of the fuselage. I don't know whether you have any conception of just how cold it is up there. What would have happened was that the clock would have frozen solid, and thus de-activate the mechanism. A real, amateur job. And thank God for it. However," and his tone became sharp again, "that doesn't change anything. We still have a bomb attempt, and a bunch of lunatics to identify and locate. They've done it once, and they'll try again."

I still didn't like him, but at least I could now understand his position. The world is full of screwballs, and the unfortunate Witchley had the unenviable task of tracking these O.P.A. people, whoever they might be.

"Tell me Mr. Witchley," I asked politely, "why didn't Florence catch that plane? She's been planning this trip for weeks, and she is one lady who sticks to what she says. Believe me, I'm in a position to know."

He scratched briefly at the side of his face.

"According to her statement," he told me, "her mother had one of her attacks. Something to do with her heart, I believe. She claims there is a long medical history there. We haven't been able to catch up with her doctor yet, but he will know the truth of it. Or otherwise."

"There isn't any otherwise," I assured him. "Florence lives with her mother, and I can think of half a dozen times in the last couple of years when she had to stay home and take care of her."

"H'm," Witchley from me to Murray Klein. "Well, where is it?"

He held out a hand. I didn't know what he was talking about, but he and Murray were evidently on the same wavelength. My lawyer friend dived into his slim leather case, and produced a document, passing it across to the federal man. Witchley stared at it intently, nodding finally.

"It's all in order. I guess you can have the lady now. Mark you," and he looked sharply at each of us in turn, "don't leave here with the wrong impression. This won't be the end of the matter, for any of you. We shall carry on with our investigation in the usual way. There are a lot of questions to be asked yet. And you can tell

Miss Digby to forget about Boston or anywhere else, for the time being. She is confined to the city limits, strictly. And," pointing a forefinger at me, "since she is being released in your custody, it is your responsibility, Mr. Preston. If the lady puts a foot wrong, you will be hauled in. You do understand that, I trust?"

"Got it," I confirmed. "Meantime, I'll be doing a little digging on my own account."

"You will?" and he sounded disbelieving at first. Then he thought further. "Oh, yes. You're a private investigator, of course. I'm sure you mean well, but you'd do better to stay out of this. Every law agency in the state of California will be working on this. I don't imagine there's much you can contribute."

I stood up, and Murray Klein did the same.

"Florence Digby," I told the federal, "is not just any old employee. She's also my friend. Somebody tried to kill her today. You don't seriously imagine I'm going to do nothing about it?"

He spread his hands.

"I can't stop you, of course. Who knows, you might even come up with something. If you do, I'd be grateful if you'd let me know. In fact, I'd be downright ungrateful if you didn't. I think you take my meaning?"

I understood him alright.

"You'll be the first," I assured him. "You understand that I may belt one or two people over the head, in the natural course of events."

He very nearly smiled. Nearly.

"Just so long as there's enough left for me to lock up."

"You got it."

"All right then. If you gentlemen will wait out at the desk, I'll see that Miss Digby is brought to you."

Everybody nodded at everybody else, and Murray and I went back through the orderly confusion, taking our seats on a wooden bench close to the station sergeant's desk.

"What do you make of it, Murray?" I asked, in low tones.

"Blessed if I know," he admitted. "There's so many of these freak terrorist outfits around these days, I couldn't claim to know them all. But this O.P.A., this is a new one on me."

"Me too," I grumbled. "Tell you something else. It's alright for me to go shouting off my mouth at that Witch-hunt, or whatever his name was, but the fact is, I wouldn't even know where to start looking. I mean, how does a man contact these weirdos?"

Murray chuckled.

"I don't see what's so funny," I complained.

"You're not sitting in my chair," he reminded. "I've never actually seen you frustrated before. If this was a nice bank robbery, or a little straightforward thuggery, you'd be off before the starting gun. Punching heads, shouting at people. You'd get some kind of result, even if it was only the wrong end of a beating. But this one is right outside your experience. Mine too, for that matter although for different reasons. It's the easiest thing in the world to plant a bomb in an airplane, if you really have the determination. I wonder what they want?"

"Who?"

I looked up quickly to see who was coming.

"No, nobody here. I mean these O.P.A. people. When this kind of thing happens there's usually a message to go with it. You know, like we want six million in gold bars, plus free tickets to Bolivia. Or the other kind, the kind who say, 'we are doing this because of the wrongful imprisonment of John Doe, the axe murderer'."

"Maybe they did," I pointed out. "That guy in there wasn't giving much away, I'll say that for him."

"Tell you what," suggested Murray. "I have a buddy, guy who was at law school with me. He's on special assignment to the D.A.'s office at the present time. He gets to hear things. Maybe I'll give him a call in the morning." If his tone had been muted before, it was positively bass register now. "You may not be aware of this, but the D.A. has a special unit these days, concentrating on anti-terrorist activities. It could be I might at least get to know the aims and objects of these people."

And even perhaps, although he didn't say as much, a couple of names to go along with it. It was a handsome offer, and I appreciated it. I said so.

"I'd certainly appreciate that. Just call me, and if you have anything, I'll come running."

We had to cut the chatter then, because Florence Digby was making her way towards us. Her appearance shocked me. I'd never known her to be any other way than neat and tidy, a woman in full possession of herself. At that moment, she looked to be in a state of semi-shock. Her clothes were rumpled, her normally immaculate hair was a disaster area, and altogether she was one lady in need of some support.

Murray sprang to her side, and I took the other arm.

"Oh Mr. Preston, Mr. Klein, I just don't know," she mumbled, "I simply don't know, I feel so ashamed. Those awful men. The things they said to me. I mean, you wouldn't believe it could happen. And poor mother is home alone. She'll be so frightened."

"It's O.K. Florence, it's all over," I muttered feeling awkward. "What's going to happen is this. I'm going to take you home now, and we'll see about getting someone to come and sit with you and your mother, maybe even stay with you. Just for tonight."

"Oh no," she protested, "I couldn't possibly. I'll be fine, once I can get into my own home, and just sit quietly for a while. There's no need."

"Sorry, it's out of our hands," I told her brusquely. "Isn't that right Mr. Klein?"

"Absolutely," he confirmed. "And I

know the very lady. She's a friend of my wife's, who happens also to be a qualified nurse, and I'll be very surprised if she isn't at your home within an hour."

We were outside now, and had reached my car. I made Florence comfortable, then closed the door and turned to the little lawyer.

"I won't forget what you did tonight, Murray. You really think you might persuade your wife's friend to do all that?"

"Tell you the truth, she's not my wife's friend at all. She does this kind of work professionally. But I do know her, and she's a very pleasant, homey sort of person, ideal for this situation. I thought Miss Digby would react more favorably to the idea of it all being kept in the family."

A smart judge of character, my friend Klein. The mention of a professional nurse would have given Florence the jitters even worse than they already were.

I suddenly remembered that the Oscar Peterson tickets were in my pocket, and Murray was an enthusiast.

"Here."

I produced the pink squares from my pocket and passed them to him. He took them in puzzlement, reading the legend.

"But these are for tonight," he said, not quite comprehending. "You're a lucky man. I tried everywhere to get seats for this show, but it's been sold out for weeks."

"Look at it this way," I suggested. "that show starts at eight o'clock, and I haven't even been able to fix up a date, what with all this hassle. Now, I have to take Florence home, and I'll kind of hang around there until your nurse arrives. There's no way I'm going to make it by eight o'clock. You now, you're different. You have a date, full-time, with a swell looking dish by the name of Ruby, sometimes known as Mrs. Klein. If you don't spend too much time jabbering with me, you can make it easily. You'll be doing me a favor."

He was undecided, possibly for three seconds. Then he grinned.

"Well, I can't stand around here, yapping it up with every passer-by. I have a show to make. First, I'll deal with that nurse problem, don't worry. Call you tomorrow."

"Give my love to Ruby."

"No chance," he refuted. "I don't like the way she looks at you now. After this, I'll probably have to chain her up."

He rushed off, a man with a schedule.

I walked slowly around the car, and climbed in beside the silent Florence.

It wasn't at all the kind of evening I'd planned.

2

THERE are people in this world who just naturally come on strong from the moment they get out of bed in the mornings. I am not one of their number. In my case the only thing that is strong is the coffee. I come on later. On that following morning I had to put in an appearance at the office early. Having insisted that Florence D. should remain at home with her mother until she'd recovered from her ordeal, it was my job to be there to welcome her so-called replacement. I slouched into the elevator with a bunch of other happy workers, and stared at my feet. As the doors began to close there was a small commotion as a late arrival squeezed through the diminishing aperture. Looking up to see what all the disturbance was about,

I noticed that the other men around me were suddenly standing more upright, pulling in their middles and assuming forceful, manly expressions. The cause of all this lethargy-shedding was a tall striking girl, with glorious raven hair, and a face straight off a magazine cover. Because of the people between us, I could only just see her from the shoulders up, and she seemed to be wearing the upper half of a lemon-colored suit, revealing a slender, bronzed throat. Being a big detective and all, I was prepared to deduce that she was also wearing the lower half of the suit, which I would probably never get to see. She would undoubtedly get off before me, and I would be left with this mental image of half a girl, to haunt me the rest of the day, perhaps all my life. I had a vision of myself as an old man, sitting in my bath-chair half a century later, with the memory of the half-girl, and trying to imagine the rest of her. It was the first time I'd ever felt any identification with the historians in the museums, faced with only a bust of some long-gone Caesar and having to complete the figure from their own imaginings.

The elevator stopped at One, and some people got out, but we were still packed in like sardines. Raven Top was still with us. At Two we lost a few more, but they were replaced by incomers, so I was no better off. Well, at Three I would have to push past her to get out, so maybe the day wouldn't be entirely wasted. The doors slid soundlessly apart, and to my astonishment she stepped out, walking away. I hurried after her, not getting too close. I wanted to see what the rest of her looked like, and it was well worth the looking. The lemon skirt ended just below the knee, and she walked with a confident, flowing grace that was an object lesson for all those hopeful kids who parade the catwalks in the Miss Whosit contests.

I was anxious to see which of my neighbours she was calling on, so that

I could make up some excuse later for dropping in for another look at her. Coffee, I decided, that would be it. My machine had broken down, and I'd come to beg a cup. Studying each painted legend as she paraded along, she passed the realty people, the architect, then the insurance company. At the fourth door she paused, checked the legend again, and knocked once, trying the handle.

I knew that legend. It read 'Mark Preston Investigations', and dream-girl was actually waiting to see me. The need for dawdling was past, and I hurried up to where she stood, yanking keys from my pocket. Smiling at her encouragingly, I said, "Good morning. Please come in."

She half-smiled, and pretended not to notice while I put in the wrong key, found the right one, and stood back to allow her to lead the way. She went in trailing a faint cloud of some fresh, light perfume.

"Are you Mr. Preston?" she queried.

The voice was low and well-modulated.

Turning in the middle of the office, she gave me an enquiring look, and an opportunity to study her face-on for the first time. Knock-out. There was no other word for her.

"Yes," I confirmed, closing the door. "I'm Mark Preston. What can I do for you?"

She held out her hand, and I took it gladly. I'd have taken the whole package given the slightest encouragement.

"I'm Candy Sullivan," she explained. "From the agency?"

In the usual way, I don't go in much for candy, but I could see that was going to have to be changed. As indeed was my prejudiced view of agency replacements.

"Glad to know you Miss Sullivan. My secretary — "

"Oh please," and she leaned her head appealingly to one side. "Do call me Candy. After all, we are going to be working together."

Florence Digby had worked for me

for a long time, but she was seldom anything but Miss Digby, especially around the office. I was going to have to get things more up-to-date around here.

"Fine," I agreed. "Candy it is. And you must call me Mark."

A look of near-horror sprang to the sculptured cheeks.

"Oh no," she protested, "that wouldn't do at all. You are my employer, after all. No, I shall call you Mr. Preston. Now then, what exactly are my duties?"

Duties, yes. I'd been wondering about that before I ever saw her. Then, she had been simply a nail-filer, a picker up of telephones. Faced with the reality of Candy Sullivan, I realised I ought to have given the matter more thought.

"Well now, let's see." Bending down, I scooped up the mail and newspapers from the floor. "This is where you will sit, and that door there leads into my own office. Perhaps it would be better if we went in there, and had a talk. I'll bring in this stuff, and we can go through it together."

"Fine."

Walking behind the Digby desk, she put down her green crocodile purse, scooped up a notepad and pencil, and looked around.

"Your secretary seems to be a very tidy person," she observed. "I've seldom been in an office where everything was so well-ordered."

I could listen to that voice all day, but obviously I was expected to make a contribution now and then.

"Yes," I agreed heartily. "Miss Digby, er Florence that is, she is very methodical. The only one around here who makes the place untidy is me. Shall we go through. Oh, by the way, the coffee machine is right there. All you have to do is switch it on."

She smiled, the way anybody would at some half-wit who found it necessary to explain that machines need switching on. I'd feel in more control of the situation, once I reached the safety of my own room. I went in first, got behind the immaculate desk and parked. Candy followed me, then stood still, and I realised she was trying to make up her mind about closing the door. A girl who looked the way she looked would have acquired a certain degree of caution in that direction.

"Leave the door open, would you mind?" I asked casually, "Otherwise, we could have a visitor out there without knowing it."

"Good," she announced mysteriously. Then she crossed over, and seated herself carefully on the other side of the desk, smoothing at her skirt, and revealing just exactly the right amount of knee.

"What's good?" I queried.

She waved elegant fingers towards the half-open door.

"That suggests to me that this job might last a little longer than some," she replied. "Working for an agency has many advantages for someone like me, but you'd be surprised how many jobs I've had to quit before nine-thirty in the morning. The grab and paw brigade are responsible, and it begins to look as though you're not a member."

I was undecided whether this was an unqualified approval, or if there might be some reflection on my virility.

"Know what you mean," I assured her, "but this is working time, so you're perfectly safe with me. If we happen to bump into each other outside of working hours, we would have a whole new situation. Does that clear your mind?"

That should do it, I decided. It wouldn't do to have a dish like this thinking there was anything wrong with me in that area. She rewarded me with a slow smile, revealing gleaming even teeth, which looked even whiter against the tanned mouth.

"I would say that is good news," she answered. "Now then, where do we start? I never worked for an investigator before. What is it you investigate exactly?"

That provided an opening for us to start talking, and in the process I began to learn more about her. Her real job was modelling, which came as no surprise. But work was scarce, and also there were a lot of people around who put their own interpretation on the word, and Candy Sullivan was not available for those activities. So, she decided that she would acquire office skills, to fill in the gaps between assignments, and as it turned out, she was good at it. An expert typist and shorthand writer, she could also operate every kind of office machine, and had even managed to pick up a little computer knowledge on the way. The reason she worked for the agency, she explained, was that the jobs were usually on a day-to-day basis, and she could always drop out if some photographer needed her. My new assistant had evidently got it all together, in addition to the fashion plate appearance. After a few minutes, during which we got to know a little about each other, I decided she'd have to be told about Florence Digby. With only two people working together, it was going to be difficult to prevent her finding out anyway, as the day wore on. There would certainly be phone calls, quite possibly visitors, and I knew from past experience that it's a near impossibility to keep a major matter completely secret in a two-room operation like mine.

"Did you hear about the bomb attempt out at the airport?" I began.

"Yes," she said, looking serious. "I caught it on the newscast. Some bunch of lunatics by the sound of it. Wasn't it lucky that the airplane didn't take off? Think of all those poor people."

"Right," I nodded. "One of those people was supposed to have been the lady you're replacing here, Miss Digby."

The finely-arched eyebrows raised in surprise.

"Really? What happened?"

I told her the bare bones of the story. I left out Agent Witchley's accusation that Murray Klein and myself might belong to this O.P.A. outfit. No point in painting any such thoughts in the mind of this decorative female. That wasn't at all the kind of image I wanted to build.

"That poor woman," she commiserated, "what a terrible ordeal. She must have been out of her mind with worry. She was lucky though."

"Lucky?"

She nodded vigorously.

"Why, certainly. In more ways than one. She might have been killed, in the first place. Then, when the police began to be unpleasant with her, she had you to call on, and you knew what to do about it. I would most certainly say she was lucky. Oh dear."

Just as I was basking in the idea of being someone people were lucky to know, some of the shine went out of her eyes.

"What's the matter?"

"I just thought," she replied, "the agency said I'd be here two days. But if your Miss Digby is still in the city, you probably won't need me tomorrow."

This kind of defeatist thinking had to be dealt with, and at once.

"Of course I shall need you tomorrow," I insisted. "Miss-er — Florence is in no shape to return to work. And besides, there's her mother's health to be considered. That lady will need looking after for the next few days. No, I'm afraid you're stuck with me, Candy. Think you'll survive?"

It got very warm in the office when she smiled.

"I'll put a brave face on it," she assured me.

I was about to make some crack about hanging on to the one she already had, when I remembered our deal about working hours.

"Fine. Well, let's see what goodies the mailman brought."

I don't usually get to see the mail, unless there's something Miss Digby thinks is worth sending in. Mostly, it splits into two categories, junk and boring, and today looked like being no exception. I had been personally selected by one company to join a special tour to Europe, including a genuine medieval dinner at a genuine English castle, not to mention a look at Napoleon's tomb, and a two-day winefest down the Danube. At twenty two hundred dollars it was a steal, but I had to return the enclosed application within thirty days. I placed the enclosed application in the waste basket, where it was shortly joined by a correspondence course in the art of detection — huh — and a special bumper bargain offer from Honest Harry Hermann, The Best Used Cars in Town. There were a couple of circular notices from insurance companies, one about a big jewel-robbery somewhere up-state, the other concerning a skip-trace job on a man who'd abandoned his wife and two adoring children without so much as a farewell. In the ordinary way, that wouldn't have bothered the company, but it seemed this particular guy had also forgotten to say farewell to the people he worked for, and had taken twelve thousand dollars in cash with him for expenses. By the way of compensation for the wife and adoring children he appeared to have taken along an eighteen year old girl from the same office.

As I scanned these things, I passed them over to the waiting Candy for inspection. It might be routine to me, and boring with it, but she was lapping it up. As she studied the color photograph of the missing gems, her eyes sparkled.

"Just imagine," she enthused, "to think that one woman actually owns all this stuff. Where will you start looking?"

"Looking?"

"Why, of course. There's a twenty thousand dollar reward. It says so right here. Or have you some bigger case on at the moment?"

I was beginning to learn that my new assistant, who was the last word in sophistication as to appearance, had also a touch of the ingenuous about her.

"That little notice," I informed her gently, "has gone to every law enforcement agency in the state, plus a few of the larger ones across the country. As to looking for it, I'd simply be wasting my time. What I'll do, today or tomorrow, is to drop into a few bars, mention that the stuff is missing, and if anybody would like to talk to me about it, my number is in the book."

Her disappointment was plain.

"And that's all?"

"That's all," I assured her. "I get something like that at least once a week. If I'm lucky, I might come up with the answer once a year, at the outside. Aren't you going to ask me about the other one? The disappearing Romeo?"

She picked up the other flier, and studied the photographs quickly.

"No," she decided. "There's no point in looking for those two. They'll be whooping it up in some vacation resort, or possibly playing the machines in Las Vegas. This girl will leave him flat, as soon as the money runs out. That could be two or three weeks. After that, he'll probably go home and face the music. I'd say it was a waste of time looking for these two."

She looked across to get my reaction, which was one of mild astonishment. Candy Sullivan evidently knew a lot more about people than she did about stolen rocks.

"You're probably right," I agreed. "We'll just file it away with the rest, and quietly forget it."

The telephone rang, and a woman's voice said, "Mr Preston? This is Mrs. Durrant."

That was the nurse. Murray Klein had arranged to look after the Digby household.

"Oh good morning," I greeted, "how are things over there, Mrs. Durrant?"

She reported that things had quietened down, and that Florence was fully recovered from her ordeal.

There wasn't any real need for her to remain there any longer, but would I mind if she made a suggestion.

"Be glad to hear it," I said.

"Well, I don't think Mrs. Digby is well enough to be left alone," she confided, "not for the next couple of days. I really think her daughter should stay home to look after her."

"Can she hear you at the moment?" I asked.

"No, she's upstairs with her mother, I wanted to have this word in private."

"I'm very glad you did, and thank you for all you've done, Mrs. Durrant. Let me suggest how to handle it. Don't tell Miss Digby you called me. Tell her I called you, asked your professional opinion, and then left instructions that she is to remain at home, at least over the coming weekend. Will you do that?"

She said she would, and I said fine,

and would she also send me her bill to the office, and she would do that to and we parted with expressions of mutual goodwill. I put down the phone and looked at Candy.

"That was the nurse," I explained, "the one at Miss Digby's house. You heard what I said."

"Yes. So, it looks as if we have to put up with each other for the next two days."

I smiled, controlling the fangs.

"I think I could just about stand that, if it's all right with you."

"Suits me, Mr. Preston. I think I'm going to like it here. Well, what do I do now?"

I picked up the newspapers and handed them across the desk.

"You read the papers," I announced.

"That's all?"

"Not quite. You're looking for anything in the way of criminal activities. Burglaries, court reports, car thefts, anything. Then you cut out the item, paste it on a sheet of paper, and bring it all back in here for me to look at later."

She stood up, giving me a mock salute.

"Like some coffee?"

"Thank you, yes. Black, no sugar."

She walked out the door, bearing her precious newspapers, and I lit an Old Favorite while I tried to put her out of my mind. Well, not entirely out, just nearer the back. When she brought in the coffee I asked her to flick over the telephone in the outer office so that people couldn't get through to me without her clearance. She liked that, and went happily away, leaving me to think.

The advent of Candy Sullivan, delicious as she was, may have raised my spirits, but it hadn't altered the thinking I'd arrived at finally in the course of a restless night. The nonsense about the grilling of Florence Digby by Agent Witchley and his kith had provoked me into an angry reaction which I had regarded, and regarded still, as entirely natural. It was only later, after I had left the Digby Family in the safe hands of Nurse Durrant, that the full import of it all began to register.

These O.P.A. people had to be found. These nut organisations seem to bloom lately like the flowers in May, but up until now they had simply been news items, so far as I was personally concerned.

The events of the previous day had changed that.

I was now involved, so far as people like Witchley were concerned. My name had been used, I had been interviewed. I was in it, however innocently or ignorantly, and I didn't like it. With so much underlying fear in the community at large, any remote hint of a connection with a bunch like that could ruin a man. Most especially, it could ruin someone like me, because I operate under a State-controlled license, and those guys can take it away any time they choose, and without having to give a reason. I'd read all about those witch-hunts which took place in the Fifties, and some of it made nasty reading. Once a thing like that begins to roll, it's hard to stop. Somehow or other, I had to make contact with the comedians, or at least find out who they were, so I could put Witchley and his crowd on their tails.

But where to start?

Murray Klein had been right the previous night. You name some kind of skulduggery, any kind, and I know places where I can go and make noises. In my line of work, that kind of knowledge is no more than my stock in trade. These creeps were another proposition entirely. They could be young, old, rich, poor, white, black or in-between. They could be anybody. There was the bomb, of course, and I wasn't forgetting that. That had been intended to self-detonate six miles above the ground, which wouldn't leave much in the way of pieces. That being so, there was always the chance that whoever put it together didn't bother about fingerprints, and if they hadn't, the F.B.I. man would have something to work with. The clock, too. It might be possible to trace it, with the kind of resources he could command. Yes, I had to admit, the knowledge that the federals were digging into this, was a source of considerable comfort. But, knowing that somebody else is doing something positive is no way the same as doing something yourself, and I very badly wanted to do something. Preferably to somebody.

The telephone interrupted my frustrated thinking, and Candy asked whether I was available to speak to Mr. Klein. I told her to put him through, and we exchanged a few cordial remarks, especially about Nurse Durrant.

Then he said, "Oh, by the way, I managed to contact my old classmate. You remember, the one on special assignment in a certain office?"

I remembered it all right. This was the man on the D.A.'s staff. Murray wasn't being cagey with me, but merely careful about any casual wire-tap which could have been put on either or both our telephones.

"Oh that one? And how was he?"

"Great shape. Great." The words were encouraging, but not the tone in which they were uttered. "He never heard of these people, not before yesterday. There wasn't even a file on them."

"So he doesn't have any names?" I pressed, discouraged.

"Just three. Yours, mine and the lady concerned. We're it."

"That's terrific, Murray. That is really terrific. Yesterday, we all thought we were Americans. Today we're Un-Americans. Is that how it reads?"

"Now, now," he soothed, "don't go making too much of that aspect of things. These people have a real problem on their hands. They're bound to latch on to anything they can find. It doesn't mean anything, because there's no foundation for it. It won't take them long to clear us. We're not quite what they're looking for."

"We'd better just pray they do find the right guys, and quick," I returned morosely.

There was no profit in pursuing that one, so he changed the subject.

"Want to thank you for those tickets, by the way. That was one great show."

He went on and on about how great it had been, which, seeing that I'd been looking forward to being there myself, didn't do a helluva lot to cheer me up. When he finally ran out of steam I said, "You forgot something."

"What's that?"

"You forgot to say 'Ruby sends her love'." I accused him."

"Oh that? No, I didn't forget. I just didn't pass it on. Can't spare it. Go get your own Ruby."

"I should be so lucky. Well, take care, and thanks again for springing Florence."

"You got it. See you."

Great, I was now under investigation

58

as a potential terrorist. All that was needed now was for some livewire newshound to sniff out what was going down, and then my troubles would really begin.

Candy Sullivan popped her welcome face around the door.

"While you were busy with Mr. Klein, another call came through. He wanted you to call back. Said it was important and urgent."

That sounded like a case, and I didn't want it. My hands were about to be occupied full-time with my own troubles. But I'd better return the call, explain to the guy that I was tied up.

"Who was it?"

"Another lawyer. We seem to be doing well for lawyers this morning." She smiled, and I found myself smiling back. "His name is Fontaine, J. J. Fontaine. I have the number."

"Did he give you any idea of what it's about?"

"No, he wouldn't go that far," she demurred, "but he was quite certain you would be very interested in what he had to say. At first, he didn't want to talk to me at all, but then I think he had the impression you were simply refusing all calls, and so he expanded a little."

I grinned. I knew what she meant. When she said the man had that impression, what she meant was she'd given him to understand that she was the first line of defense, and nobody got through without a reason.

"That was nice of him," I conceded. "What did he expand about?"

"Nothing in detail. All he would say was that it had a strong connection with a certain story which was on the front page of every newspaper, and I was to make that point to you. I have all the papers on my desk, Mr. Preston, and there's only one story which is on every front page. It's the bomb attempt, naturally."

Naturally. I was immediately very interested in Mr. J. J. Fontaine.

"Fontaine, Fontaine," I muttered.

"Nope, I don't believe I ever heard of him. He didn't tell you what kind of law he's in, did he?"

"No." She shook her head, and the raven hair gleamed in the morning sunlight. "But I looked into it, while you were busy with Mr. Klein. It seems that our Mr. Fontaine does not practise general law. He works on a retainer basis only, for just a handful of special clients."

There was more to this girl than the way she walked.

"And just how the devil did you manage to find that out?" I queried.

She looked happily mysterious.

"Oh, working for an agency has its advantages. A girl gets around a lot, meeting all kinds of people. It's surprising how many friends you can make, if you take the trouble. I just made a couple of phone calls, and voila! I got the answer in the end."

I could just bet she did, too.

"Maybe we should swap chairs," I suggested. "You seem to be quite

61

an investigator in your own right. I shouldn't be surprised if you have his list of clients as well. Do you?"

"I'm afraid not. But I think you ought to call him, don't you? I mean, if he has any information about this outrage — "

" — then he shouldn't be telling me," I cut in. "He ought to be telling the State Prosecutor's Office, the D.A., somebody in an official capacity. He shouldn't be confiding in some broken-down gumshoe."

She laughed then. It was the first time I'd heard her, and I hoped it wouldn't be the last. A pleasant, throaty sound, warm.

"Mr. Preston, please don't insult my intelligence with that routine," she ordered. "Broken down indeed. That tie alone must have cost you twenty dollars at least. You have an apartment at Parkside Towers, which is not exactly a slum clearance area, and the rental on these offices is paid up for the next twelve months."

"Ah," I remonstrated. "But you don't know how much I owe the bookies."

"No, I don't," she confessed. "You want me to look into it?"

"No," I replied hastily. "Please don't bother. It's bad enough that I should know. Let's stick to one thing at a time. If this Fontaine really wants to talk about this bomb thing, then I certainly want to listen. Will you get him for me, please?"

She got him for me please, and I arranged to be at his house in thirty minutes. I wondered why I should go there instead of his office, but I didn't ask any questions. That could come later.

On the way out, I said to Candy.

"I've no idea how long this'll take. Florence usually goes to lunch from 12.30 till one, but you suit yourself."

"I don't eat lunch," she informed me. "but I may go out for a while, stare in shop windows."

"Whatever suits you. See you later."

I left her there, cutting up newspapers.

3

WHATEVER kind of law it was that J. J. Fontaine practised, it certainly seemed to pay well enough. The house was a twenty-minute drive from the city centre, a mock-Tudor structure standing well back from the road in secluded, well-tended grounds. If Mr. Fontaine decided to move, he would be asking for four hundred thousand, and closing at three hundred fifty, so he ought to be able to meet my reasonable charges without selling any heirlooms.

The door chimes produced a formidable lady in her middle years, very correct as to her dress and general deportment.

"Would you be Mr. Preston?"

I confirmed that I would, and she invited me into the cool hallway.

"If you will please wait just a

moment, I will advise Mr. Fontaine that you have arrived."

I didn't think she was Mrs. Fontaine, more an office-type lady, and this was confirmed within less than a minute. She appeared back at the doorway through which she had first exited, beckoning me to come in. I went into a small room that was obviously an outer office, complete with typewriter and the rest of the paraphernalia. Another door stood open in the opposite wall. She motioned me through, closing the door behind me, and presumably returning to her duties.

A man was standing by open french windows, waiting for me. He was tall and spare, with a shock of white hair above a well-tanned clean-shaven face, amazingly clear of lines. I guessed him to be about sixty years old, looking every day of forty five. He was informally dressed, and there was a pleasant smile on his face as he came toward me, hand outstretched.

"How do, Mr. Preston. Good of you to come."

His voice was soft and mellifluous, the handshake mercifully dry. I returned his greeting, taking in the rich furnishings of the library cum office in which we were standing.

"Please sit down, Mr. Preston. I was about to indulge in a glass of iced lemonade. Perhaps you'll join me?"

I nodded my thanks and parked in a hardbacked chair facing the ancient desk. The severe lady appeared almost at once, with a jug that clanked of ice as she set down the silver tray. Then she carefully poured out two glasses, one for the master of the house, one for me.

"Thank you, Myrtle. Will you please see that we are not disturbed for the next twenty minutes?"

"Very well Mr. Fontaine."

She gave me a half-smile on her way out, so I gave her half of one of mine. I hadn't met anyone called Myrtle in years.

"Here's to our understanding," saluted Fontaine, sipping at his drink.

I didn't know what it was we were supposed to be understanding, but I nodded encouragingly and swallowed some of the lemonade.

"Have you any idea of who I am, or what I do?" he began.

"Not really," I admitted. "I know you're an attorney of some kind, and I believe you have quite a restricted practise — "

" — Oh?" he butted in. "Who told you that?"

I put on what I like to think is my enigmatic expression.

"You forget Mr. Fontaine, I'm supposed to be a private investigator. A man in my line of work ought to know something about his own city, wouldn't you say? That is, if he's any good."

He nodded, considering this. I knew he was sizing me up, getting the feel of me, if you like, and I was doing the same for him. He'd told Candy Sullivan this interview would connect somehow with what happened the previous day out at the airport. It just didn't fit that J. J. Fontaine would have any link with the Oppressed Peoples of America, or anywhere else. He wasn't doing too much suffering from where I was sitting.

"Yes, I suppose that is a reasonable answer," he decided finally. "One does one's best to keep a low profile, but at the same time one can scarcely conceal the fact that one exists."

One could not, and I grinned encouragingly.

"That was a very nasty business yesterday," he went on, almost offhandedly. "A lot of people might have lost their lives."

"It isn't very often that anyone has cause to be grateful for the smog," I replied, "but I guess yesterday was an exception."

"Quite. Quite so. I understand you were involved in the affair, remotely of course. I mean that one of your staff was due to take that particular flight."

Low profile or no, Mr. Fontaine seemed to have his own ear close to the ground.

"That's right," I agreed. "My secretary, a Miss Digby. How did you come to know that, Mr. Fontaine?"

"I don't believe that is especially relevant," he said, brushing the question aside. "The point is, the lady cancelled her reservation at the last moment. Would you happen to know why?"

My instinct was to tell him to mind his own business, but I held it back. I'd made the trip out to learn, not to start arguments. Besides, it was a fair bet that if he knew so much already, then he probably also knew the answer to his own question. Pretending a kind of respectful reluctance I said, "Her mother has a heart condition, and one of her attacks came on a couple of hours before flight-time. I don't want to seem impolite, Mr. Fontaine, but what makes it any of your concern?"

I thought he might take offense at the question, but he accepted it calmly.

"A fair point," he conceded, "and I will answer you in a few moments. First of all, I should like to ask another question. Are you intending to take any action in the matter?"

Action? What was he driving at? For a fleeting moment I wondered whether, as a lawyer, he might be offering his services in an action against the authorities for wrongful detention, or harassment, or whatever. But I got rid of the thought as quickly as it came. That was for those new boys, the hot-shots, the ambulance chasers. People in his position didn't have to grub around in those areas. But the word he had used was action, so if it wasn't legal action he must mean something a little more positive. My kind of action.

"I would certainly like to," I told him, picking my words. "The trouble is, I don't know who these people are, or where to start looking for them. I don't mind telling you, Mr. Fontaine, I'm pretty frustrated about it."

It seemed to be more or less what he expected to hear, to judge by the expression on his face.

"According to my sources," he went on, "you are a man who likes to get results. These same sources tell me that you sometimes achieve these by, what shall we say, methods which would not accord with the strictest interpretation of the law. Would that be too strong?"

I shook my head, conscious of a growing feeling that this journey would prove to be worthwhile.

"No, I don't think that's too strong. Sometimes, the law is helpless, even though the answer is plain. I don't mind breaking a few rules, if things are going to come out right in the end."

"Or a few heads, either, I'm told."

He made it a statement. I shrugged.

"It's a hard world."

He sipped soundlessly at his frosted glass, eyeing me over the rim.

"How did you get along with Agent Witchley?"

The question seemed casual, but I knew it wasn't. There was nothing casual about J. J. Fontaine.

"Not too well, at first," I admitted. "I was pretty sore about the way they hauled in Florence — Miss Digby, that is — but when I calmed down, I could see the man had a job to do."

"Did he warn you to stay away from the enquiries?" he wanted to know.

"He tried," I answered, "But I guess he could tell I wouldn't take any notice. The last thing he said was that if I came up with anything, I'd better let him know, or I'd regret it."

"Capital," he breathed. "So if I understand you correctly, no one is going to be very surprised if they find you ferreting around, asking questions?"

"No," I assured him. "They might not like it, but they won't be surprised. Quite the reverse, in fact, so far as the local police are concerned. Knowing that my Miss Digby could have blown up with that airplane, they would think it odd if I wasn't around, sticking my nose into everything."

"May one ask why?" he queried, soft eyes searching my face. "Miss Digby could scarcely afford your fees, I imagine? So perhaps there's something else which would prompt you to move? Forgive me if this sounds indelicate, but is this lady perhaps something more than a mere employee?"

I knew what he was getting at, and there was no point in resenting it. From his standpoint, as an outsider, it was a fair question.

"Much more," I confirmed. "But not in the way you imply, Mr. Fontaine. The lady is my good and loyal friend, and I don't like people who cause trouble for my friends."

"So there's not an emotional involvement," he seemed to be talking to himself "better and better."

It was his house, and his lemonade,

but I'd had enough of this cross-examination.

"I seem to be answering a lot of questions," I pointed out, "But you still haven't got around to what I'm doing here."

"Patience, Mr. Preston," he advised, "I don't think that you'll find that I'm wasting your time. It is simply that I have to be satisfied in my own mind about these preliminaries."

Well, that sounded promising, at least. After the preliminaries, they have to put on the main event. We could be getting somewhere at last. I kept quiet now, while he got his thoughts in order.

"Now then, as I understand it, the situation is this," he began, like a judge summing up for a jury. "Your employee, in fact your very good friend, narrowly escaped with her life, as a result of the activities of this so-called O.P.A. group. But you are not just any employer. You happen to be a private investigator, a rather well-known one, and it would be in your nature, to use your own expression, to be sticking your nose into everything. No one will be at all surprised when you do."

That's what he said. 'When' you do. Not 'if'.

"That's it exactly," I confirmed.

"Then I think I might now come to the point," he decided. "Incidentally, just so there is no legal misunderstanding between us, you will please consider yourself as being consulted on a professional basis from the moment you left your office to come here. That makes me your client, and this entire conversation is confidential within the terms of your license, and the laws of the state in relation to that license. Understood?"

I understood all right. He was telling me that if I started blabbing about whatever it was he was about to say, he'd yank strings to have my sticker pulled. That was twice I'd been threatened that way inside of twenty four hours. First Witchley, now him.

I didn't like it any better the second time than I had the first.

"In that case," I shot back. "You must understand that I have a three-day minimum fee."

"Perfectly acceptable," he assured me, unperturbed.

"Whether I take the job or not," I emphasised.

"Still acceptable," he returned coolly, "although I think there is very little likelihood of your refusing. In fact you would be a fool to do so. And, Mr. Preston even on this short acquaintance, I do not categorise you as a fool."

It was some kind of compliment, so I inclined my head.

"What do you know of the precious stone trade, Mr. Preston?" he asked sharply.

I made a doubtful face.

"Haven't had much to do with it," I confessed. "I've been involved in the recovery of stolen property a few times, it's all on the files. But I couldn't claim any knowledge of the legitimate trade. I hear tales, of course."

He leaned forward slightly, interested.

"Tales? Tell me about these tales," he urged.

"Well, it's only hearsay," I said. "I hear that the big operators work on trust. A man walks into another man's office, with a pocketful of stones, they agree a price, and the visitor goes away. He doesn't take any cash, just a handshake. Then the new owner goes through the same routine with other people. Everybody trusts everybody else, and it all works out. It all sounds crazy to me, but that's the way I hear it."

After listening intently, he smiled slightly, and the corners of his eyes lifted.

"A trifle over-simple, if you'll pardon my saying so, but basically yes. You have the right general idea, and certainly the central theme is entirely accurate. Trust is everything. It would no more occur to a genuine dealer to betray that trust than it would to — to betray his country. Yes, I think I may put it as strongly as that. And this is not a local matter, not even a national one. The trade is world-wide, with Amsterdam being, of course, the world center as you know. A narrow world within a world, where everyone knows everyone else, at least by name. You mentioned earlier that I have a very few clients, and you were absolutely right. I represent the precious stone trade in this part of the State, for one thing. And that is why you are here."

"I see."

I didn't see at all, but he'd get to it when he was ready.

"Does the name Keane mean anything to you?" he queried "Walter M. Keane?"

Nothing registered, so I shook my head.

"No. What does he do? Should I know him?"

"Indeed not. I should have been rather disappointed if you had said anything else. Mr. Keane is also a man of very low profile. Tell me, did you manage to see the passenger list on Flight 147 for yesterday afternoon?"

It couldn't have been good for my neck muscles, to have to keep rotating them sideways like that.

"No, I didn't."

"Had you done so, you would have found the name of Walter M. Keane on the list. He too, has reason to be thankful to our smog. Even more than your Miss Digby, because he was actually aboard the plane, waiting for the take-off."

"Then he's a lucky man," I commented.

"In one way, yes. Let us change the subject for a moment, and return to the business of the bomb."

I shrugged in acquiescence. It might be my time, but he was now paying for it. He could spend it any way he chose.

"As we know, the telephone warning was received at 16.15 hours. The caller stated that the device would explode at 16.30. A margin of only fifteen minutes, Mr. Preston, at most."

"At most?"

"Certainly, These things are unreliable. For all the authorities knew, it could have gone off at any second. Besides which, they had no way of knowing whether the caller was telling the truth. They had no time for niceties. They ordered emergency evacuation, and very properly so. There was no time for running out stairways, and normal disembarkation. Are you familiar with the emergency evacuation process?"

"Not at first hand," I confessed. "Just what I've seen on the news. They blow out these plastic air balloon doodads, and people just slide down them. That's the only kind I've seen."

"Precisely. There is one of these devices on each side of the fuselage, probably more on the large aircraft, I really wouldn't know. We are only concerned with Flight 147. These devices were put into operation immediately, while the emergency crews were racing out to the spot. Ambulances, firemen, police. The first of these reached the scene at 16.18, just as the first of the passengers was emerging. The crew of the aircraft were magnificent, and the performance of the emergency people was beyond reproach. On the whole, the passengers themselves performed very well, but of course there was a good deal of alarm, and there were one or two regrettable incidents. A few of them panicked, and tried to push their way out ahead of their turn. A perfectly natural reaction, under the circumstances, but of course it caused a certain amount of confusion."

I could well imagine. With forty six passengers, plus a crew of four or possibly five, we were talking about a minimum of fifty people. I had no way of knowing the statistics, but it was inevitable that out of that number, a given percentage would lose their heads.

Mr. Fontaine's sonorous tones rolled on.

"There was some bumping and jostling," he continued, "but the crew members were very firm and calm. The aircraft was empty, and already being searched, by 16.22. A remarkable performance, and no praise is too high for all the services concerned. By that time, a passenger coach had arrived, and people were boarded and driven away immediately. We have to remember there was still a time-bomb to be located, and the expected explosion could well cause loss of life in the immediate vicinity of the aircraft. As I have said, there was no time for little delicacies."

That wasn't what he'd said before. Last time the word had been 'niceties', but it meant the same thing. And it was clearly important I should register the point. He hadn't made it twice for nothing.

"Now we return to Mr. Keane. He is not a person who enjoys air travel, and he is not alone in that. Some people have to take several drinks before they will even board an aircraft, others take pills of various kinds to settle their nerves. Our Mr. Keane comes into the second category. Well, almost. In his case, when undertaking a trip by air, he waits until he is safely in his seat, and ready for take-off, before he swallows a certain type of pill. It's effect lasts for only thirty minutes, normally means that the aircraft is well and truly on it's way, before the effects wear off. It is only the thought of the take-off, you see, the thought of leaving terra firma, which gives him apprehension. Once the craft is five or six miles up in the sky, he is no longer afraid. Irrational, I grant you, but by no means uncommon."

I knew the type, and as my lecturer had said, they were not at all rare. It was time I made some kind of contribution.

"I've met the type," I conceded. "So, in the case of Mr. Keane, can we assume that he would have been aboard at say ten minutes of four, and would have taken his pill right away?"

Fontaine shook his snowy head.

"No. Take-off time was scheduled for four o'clock, and he took the pill at precisely that hour. He is very clear on the point, and Mr. Keane does not make mistakes about details."

It was evident that Mr. Keane had already received a very thorough grilling on the point. Why?

"Well then, if that's the case," I put in, "he would have been in a state of mind which was, how shall I put it, less than clear when the evacuation order came through, and when he went rolling down the chute?"

The man behind the desk beamed.

"Exactly. And now, you will be wondering why Mr. Keane's foggy recollection should be of consequence."

In my mind, I had already formed a conclusion about that, but it would be better to hear it from the horse's-mouth, if you follow me.

"Yes, I'm wondering," I admitted. "It seems to be important."

"Very," he confirmed. "You see, Mr. Keane was acting as a courier for certain interests whom I represent. He had in his possession, a small flat briefcase containing a quarter of a million dollars in uncut diamonds. At some stage in the process of evacuation, Mr. Keane was jostled or pushed, and the case taken away from him. My clients, Mr. Preston, want those stones recovered."

I made a whistling sound. I could imagine they would.

"And you don't have any doubts about Keane himself?"

"None whatever," he assured me.

"I'd like to talk with him, all the same. Find out what he can remember about where he was sitting, who was closest to him, anything at all that might give us a lead."

"I'm afraid that won't be possible," he rejected. "Mr. Keane has been so upset by this entire affair that his doctors have ordered a few days rest. It will be two or three days at least before he will be available."

You could never tell with people at Fontaine's level. The words could mean exactly what they said, and the unfortunate Keane was recovering from the ordeal. On the other hand, they could also mean that he had already been asked a lot of questions by people who were accustomed to getting answers. People who used up-to-date techniques, like fists and knives and lighted matches. You just couldn't tell. Either way, it was clear that the man was incommunicado, as far as I was concerned. It was a pity, but I'd have to do the best I could.

"Well that's too bad," I commented, without inflection. "I'll just have to make do without him."

"Quite so," he purred. "I gather from that, you accept the assignment? I had rather hoped you might."

"You bet I do," I replied, and this time with enthusiasm. "This gives me exactly what I need. A genuine bona

86

fide excuse for asking a lot of questions, and I can — "

My voice tailed away, as he wagged his head in denial.

"Unfortunately, that will not be the precise situation. I cannot give you an official permit on this. In fact, the real purpose of your enquiry must remain confidential between us."

"But if your people have been robbed — " I began to remonstrate.

" — Ah yes, I take your point. But we cannot allow that to become known. As I explained to you earlier, the precious stone trade rests entirely on trust. With trust goes credibility. It is taken for granted that our couriers are safe people, that our arrangements are watertight. We cannot permit any other kind of impression to be gained."

I thought he was over-emphasising.

"In the ordinary way," I objected, "I could see the sense of that. But your people can hardly be expected to foresee that some bunch of nuts is going to plant a bomb on an airplane."

"True," he agreed, "but even that would not excuse us. Believe me, even a nuclear explosion would be regarded with suspicion. No, Mr. Preston, we cannot allow this to get out. Before we say any more, I am correct, am I not, in assuming that you will still wish to carry on with the enquiry? Given this rather major reservation?"

I considered this at length. A length of about four seconds. There was no doubt I was going to take the job, never had been, whatever the conditions. For one thing, it gave me something positive to do, something with a purpose. It was a hell of an improvement over chasing around over these madmen who called themselves the O.P.A.

"Yup," I confirmed, at mind already with possibilities. "I was intending to poke around anyway, so this will give point to it. Who knows? I might even turn up this bomb-squad and get to kick in a few teeth. I'd enjoy that."

I must have put more feeling into the words than I realised, because my new employer winced slightly.

"I trust, Mr. Preston, that you will not permit your personal involvement in this matter to cloud the main issue? Pray, don't misunderstand me. I well understand your feelings, and they do you credit. But I am not very interested in those people, except as an outraged citizen. My concern is for my clients interests, and I must ask you also to make these your first priority. There is also the matter of perspective."

He paused, inviting a question, so I asked it.

"What do you mean by that?"

Even the skin on his hands was not especially wrinkled, I noticed, as he closed them thoughtfully under his chin.

"I mean that the missing property is a reality. It has been stolen by real people, with profit in mind. This is your kind of territory, the kind of thing at which you are very experienced, and clearly successful. The other business, the political thing, if that is what it is, is shadow-chasing. Every law enforcement agency in the State, in the country, will be bringing large forces to bear in seeking out the perpetrators of this outrage. You must not take it as any reflection on your abilities when I point out that you can scarcely compete with that kind of organisation."

It didn't make any better listening, just because it happened to be the plain truth. I had to struggle with myself to force out my next words.

"I know what you are telling me is no more than the plain truth," I admitted, "But it's hard to come to terms with it. I'm not the kind of person who relishes feeling helpless, Mr. Fontaine. And I must tell you this. If I do get a line on those creeps, I'll be after them. But," I added hastily, and before he could protest, "I know that your job has to have priority. Now then, could we get down to what happens if I get lucky, and locate your property?"

He unclasped his hands, changed his

mind, and locked them together again.

"Happens?"

"Yes. What sort of reward are we talking about, bonus, if you like. I take it, although this is strictly under wraps, that the normal insurance rates will apply. That is to say, ten per cent of the face value."

In the ordinary way, I have no skill with mathematics, but I'm amazingly sharp when we're talking about reward money. Ten per cent of a quarter of a million is twenty-five thousand dollars, a sum which has a nice round ring to it.

He heard me out, then made a deprecatory gesture with his hands.

"I am aware of the insurance procedure, but this is not being dealt with through those channels. My proposition is five per cent. Twelve and a half thousand dollars, Mr. Preston. A great deal of money."

I frowned.

"It's a whole lot less than twenty-five," I objected.

"Ah yes," he agreed smoothly. "But think of the difficulties I know you must have experienced in the past, when it comes to the actual payment of money by the insurance people. How many times, for example, have they decided that you weren't entitled to the full amount, for one reason or another? How many times have they pointed out exclusion in the small print, which has had the effect of reducing the actual cash paid over to eight per cent or seven or less?"

That was close to home, and I had a long history of bitter wrangling with those people on exactly that point.

"It does happen," I admitted.

"Of course, of course. Then there is the delay in payment to be considered. Months go by, many months sometimes. And then, finally, when you do get paid, who should turn up but your dear old Uncle Sam, in the shape of the Internal Revenue. A sizeable chunk of the money is whisked away, as we all know to our cost."

I began to see what he was driving at. When you thought about it in those terms, the actuality of it was brought home.

"So you're saying — ", I began, but he flagged me down.

" — I am saying that the situation here is quite different. On the day you recover that property I shall pay you, and in cash, the sum of twelve thousand five hundred dollars. The Internal Revenue are very busy, terribly overworked as it is. I am sure neither of us wishes to add to their burden by mentioning our little transaction."

When you cut out the fancy words, he was saying that I would get twelve and a half big ones, cash in hand, and no questions asked. Put like that, it was one of those offers you hear about, the non-refusable variety.

"It's a deal, Mr. Fontaine," I agreed. "Five per cent, paid on delivery."

"Splendid. Now tell me, what can I do to help you get started?"

I'd been thinking about all kinds

of possibilities while we were talking. When I began to talk, it was little more than thinking out loud.

"We're really talking about two people here," I mused. "Your Mr. Keane, and the thief. Keane has the stones and the thief knows it. That's point one. How did he know? You don't just look at a person and think to yourself that looks like a man who could be carrying a bagful of diamonds. Somebody, somewhere, must have told him. That has to be someone in your clients' world, Mr. Fontaine, and I think they will be able to make better guesses than me as to who that informant might be. That's point one. Point two is, our thief was on the airplane, so he has to be one of the other passengers. Or a crew member, although I think that's unlikely."

That produced raised eyebrows.

"Why do you exclude the crew? The prospect of a quarter of a million dollars can seduce the most unlikely people."

"Because of the law of chance," I explained. "There was nothing to say Keane wouldn't change his mind at the last moment, take a different flight. Even go to another city altogether. Plus the fact the crews themselves can be switched at the last minute. No. I exclude them on practical grounds."

His eyes gleamed for a moment before he nodded.

"Very well. Please continue."

"There were forty six passengers aboard, including Keane. That leaves forty five, and it shouldn't take long to get that number down to a reasonable size."

"And how would you propose to do that?" he queried.

"Simple elimination. We can cut out all the elderly people, for a start. Mothers with children. Disabled people. Probably some others too, when we actually get down to cases. You see, we have one thing going for us, Mr. Fontaine, and that is the bomb. No one could have foreseen that, but it happened. When it did, our thief was able to adapt quickly. We've no way of knowing what the original intention was about robbing Mr. Keane, but it wasn't going to be done during the flight, that's for certain. No, your man would have reached his destination quite safely, and from that point on was when the thief intended to make his move. At the airport, in a cab, at the hotel Keane was headed for, who knows? Suddenly, with the bomb, our man finds himself with a whole new ballgame. He has to adapt to this new situation, scrap all the earlier plans, whatever they were. He has to be quick, active, and strong enough to get close to Keane, do whatever it was he did, and grab the case. My guess would be that we're looking for somebody aged between twenty-five and fifty. I may have to eat those words later, but that's how I intend to start."

"Why twenty-five?" he asked, with a puzzled expression.

"Because this is the big league," I

explained. "Nobody is going to trust an operation of this size to any young punk. It has to be someone with a few years of reliable experience behind them. Matter of fact, I'm stretching it a little, even at twenty-five. Thirty would probably be nearer the mark. We'll see."

Fontaine smiled slowly, leaning his head on the back of the great leather chair.

"I think I am beginning to understand how it comes about that you are able to afford that expensive apartment of yours. Yes, I think I may say, I begin to see a glimmer of hope here. One question. You seem to make the assumption that the person we want is a man. Do I take it that you rule out the possibility of a woman?"

I grinned, not too much.

"Experience has taught me that it is never a safe proposition to rule out the women in anything. They can be just as rough and tough as any man given the circumstances. No, sir, I do not exclude them at all."

"Good," he exclaimed. "I, too, have had reason in the past to be surprised by persons of the other gender. We seem to progress. And now, I think, it is time for me to hand you this."

Sliding open a drawer, he took out some sheets of paper and slid them across the desk. I bent forward to collect them, turned them the right way round, and began to read. I was looking at the passenger list for Flight 147 the previous day, with extra entries. In addition to the usual columns, the ones held by cabin staff to check in arrivals, there were columns headed 'Date of Birth', 'Nationality', 'Occupation', and very much wider, 'Comments'.

All the columns were printed except the last which had been completed in handwriting. Or rather, the original had. What I was holding was a set of photo-copies, and those comments had not been scribbled down by airways personnel. A quick scan was enough to show that most of my work, the eliminating work which was an essential pre-requisite to tracking down our thief had already been done for me. At the top, right-hand corner were the words TOP CONFIDENTIAL — TWO COPIES ONLY. I didn't have to be told that what I had in my hand was not one of those two copies. There were no other markings, nothing to identify the source of the material.

"Very impressive," I admitted. "Do you mind if I ask you how you came by this Mr. Fontaine?"

He gave me that urbane, bland look of his.

"Certainly not," he purred, "you are free to ask me anything you choose. However, you must allow me the freedom to decline an answer. Let us simply leave it that the information is genuine, and that it should make your task somewhat easier."

"Easier?" I echoed. "It would have taken me two days at least to put all this stuff together. As for these 'comment' entries, I wouldn't even know where to look for some of this stuff. You're probably quite used to impressing people, Mr. Fontaine. Well, you've done it again. I'm impressed."

One of the well-kept hands waved that away.

"You probably went to bed last night," he pointed out, "and so did I. We were the lucky ones. There was no sleep for a lot of officials until that preliminary list was produced. Time, as the saying goes, is of the essence, in a matter of this kind."

I stared down at the list again, beginning already to make mental notes of a few obvious points. Fontaine had still not finished his explanation, but I'd had all I was going to get. The unlucky investigators, who'd been working around the clock to produce the stuff in my hand, would have been less than gratified to learn that the end product of all their labour was being scanned by a certain P.I. with an official rating of nil. How my latest employer had managed to get his hands on it was neither here nor there. The important thing, at that moment, was that I'd got it.

"I'm afraid I can't allow that out of the house."

I looked up in surprise.

"But I can never memorise all this stuff," I objected.

"I appreciate that. Someone as a great personal favour to me has risked a lifetime's reputation to give me that list and I could not let it out of my hands. What I suggest is that you take it into another room and study it. Make such notes as you require, short of actually reproducing the list, and then bring it back here to me."

He must have been pushing a buzzer or something that I couldn't see, because the lady named Myrtle opened the door at that moment, and stood waiting. I got up, clutching my precious sheets.

"Myrtle will find you a quiet spot where you can work."

"Thank you. I'll be as quick as I can."

I walked out, past the waiting secretary, who pulled the door shut and motioned for me to follow her. She led me into another room, which was clearly in the private part of the house. No desks here, no bookshelves, just a quietly furnished place to sit and relax. By the open window was a small oak bureau with a farmhouse kitchen chair beside it.

"Mr. Fontaine thought you could work over there," she pointed, "I have set out notepaper and a pencil. Would there be anything else you might require, Mr. Preston?"

I assured her that this would be fine, and she went away. For a moment I stood at the window, staring at the ordered tranquility of the neat grass and shrubbery. A man certainly ought to be able to work in such surroundings, I reflected. Everything was so calm and peaceful, and there would be no distractions, except when a couple of visiting birds began a squabble over worm-rights.

Reluctantly, I turned to the bureau. It was one of those contraptions where the front drops down to be supported by two sliding arms which emerge from beneath. I sat down, placed the list in front of me, and began my scrutiny.

The list was not in alphabetical order, and had clearly been devised from the official airline list, which simply made the entries in order of booking. The first passenger was a Mrs. Julie Wallace, widow, home address in a small town one hour's drive from Boston, Mass. This lady was sixty-three years old, and, according to the notes, had come to Monkton City to visit with her daughter and son-in-law. Mrs. Wallace had booked her seat on Flight 147 a week earlier, having stayed with her family for ten days. The final entry in the 'Comments' column was terse to put it mildly. It said simply 'Clearance — Total'. That was good for Mrs. Wallace, and good for me, too. I could forget about the lady. But that final remark gave me an idea. There was no point in my wading through all this information, fascinating though it was. All I really needed was to go straight to that last entry, as a first move, then pay close attention to the people who did not receive that 'Clearance — Total' accolade.

Five minutes later I was left with only nine names, and the job was already assuming proportions I felt more able to cope with. At the forefront of my mind was the continual reminder, that the people who'd made these entries had started off from a different base-point. They were not looking for potential jewel-thieves, but for people who could not be ruled out entirely as political activists. I pondered about this for quite a while, smoking thoughtfully and resting my eyes on the lush grass. After all, a person could have first-rate political clearance, and still have crooked inclinations. I might have to go back over those 'Clearance — Total' items and have a second look at some of the entries. Meantime, I had to start somewhere. There would be enough time to think about second looks after I'd dealt with what I already had.

What I had was a potential short-list of nine candidates, and my first priority must be to deal with those, and I got off to a very promising start. Four of them were out, within my terms of reference.

The first man was a one-time movie writer, who'd been black-listed years before during one of Hollywood's clean-up campaigns. He was now seventy-six years old, and not exactly the man to fit the physical requirements I had laid down.

There were two women members of some movement whose objective was to free the American women from her enslavement to hearth and stove. Hearth and stove? Where had these characters been lately? I crossed them off.

My last pencilling-out was a man

who had started out in life as a woman, and thus failed to satisfy the previous examiners. Well, he satisfied me. I had no way of assessing what this unfortunate character must have suffered in the past, but his emotional problems must have been enormous. I could not visualise the big operators entrusting a top level job of this nature to someone with that kind of history.

That left me with five, a good manageable number. I copied out carefully every scrap of information there was about each of them, read it through again to be absolutely certain none of them could be eliminated, but came up with nothing.

No, wait a minute.

There was one thing, but for that I would need to refer back to J. J. Fontaine. Gathering up my papers, I closed the bureau carefully, and put the wooden chair back in it's place. Then I went back to the small outer office where Myrtle was typing busily away. She looked up as I entered, gave me that grave little smile again, and passed a hand over her hair.

"Finished already, Mr. Preston?"

"Well, almost," I concluded. "I would just like to have one more quick word with Mr. Fontaine before I leave."

She nodded, rising.

"Yes, he anticipated that you probably would. I am to show you straight in."

Crossing to the door of the inner sanctum, she knocked and opened it. I could see Fontaine, seated at his desk reading.

"Mr. Preston is about ready to leave," she announced, waving me inside, and leaving us alone.

Fontaine looked at his watch.

"You've been less than an hour," he pointed out. "I had imagined you would be here for quite some time."

Although he didn't come right out and say so, his tone implied that he hoped he wasn't getting a sloppy job. I hastened to correct any such impression.

"So did I," I assured him. "Let me tell you about the way I've approached the problem. Courtesy, I may say, of all the spadework done by whoever produced this list."

He nodded his agreement, and paid careful attention while I led him through my reasoning. It seemed to satisfy him, at least for the moment.

"You may have to reconsider of course," he decided, "but yes, I think I agree with your basic reasoning. And, certainly, you have to start somewhere. So now you have it down to five people? That really sounds quite hopeful."

"It does. In fact, it might be possible to reduce it even further, but only you can do that. When was the decision made that your Mr. Keane should take Flight 147?"

The few lines on his forehead knitted into an intricate pattern.

"I don't quite see — " he began.

"Let me amplify on that," I urged. "We have ruled out any possibility that there was anything accidental about this. The theft was planned in advance. Admittedly, it wasn't intended to be carried out the way it was, and our friend had to make some very quick, last-minute adjustments, to get his or her hands on those diamonds."

"Agreed. But I'm still not quite taking your point."

"The list," and I placed the sheets in front of him, "contains vital information, including the date and time the reservation was made. Mr. Keane's own entry states that his flight was reserved on Monday, at eleven a.m., but that isn't the crucial factor here. The vital point is, at what time of which day was it decided that he would catch the Boston plane on Wednesday? Because, whoever our thief is, and wherever he got his information from, he could not have made his own reservation until Mr. Keane's departure time was known. Anybody who called the airport before that time, can be crossed off the list."

"Yes." He did his hand-locking

routine again. "Yes, I like that. I like that very much indeed. I would need to make a telephone-call in order to find out what you want to know. I wonder if you would be good enough to wait outside with Myrtle while I make the call."

So there I was, outside again, with the unfortunate Myrtle unable to decide whether she could get on with her work, or whether she was expected to indulge in chit chat with me.

"Don't mind me," I encouraged. "In my job, I do a lot of waiting."

Re-assured, she lowered her head, and began clacking busily away. After about four minutes, a light glowed briefly on her desk. She smiled across at me.

"Mr. Fontaine is ready for you now."

I went back inside, making sure the door was closed. The lawyer wasted no time in getting to the point.

"The decision was reached at ten o'clock on Monday," he announced, "and as you have pointed out, the reservation was made one hour later. How does that affect your list now?"

I consulted my papers.

"That cuts out two people," I was happy to report. "One made the booking last Friday, the other on Sunday. So, Mr. Fontaine, I am left with only three."

He didn't exactly bounce with enthusiasm, but then he wasn't the bouncy type. But there was no concealing his evident pleasure.

"Splendid. Excellent. Well, Mr. Preston. I think we may begin to feel a little hopeful about all this. Here."

Reaching inside a drawer, he pulled out a thick envelope.

"One thousand dollars," he announced. "Tens, twenties and fifties. Let us call that your retainer."

I didn't care what he called it, just so I got my hands on it. He wasn't the kind of man who would have appreciated my counting it, so I stuck the whole thing in an inside pocket.

"I'll be in touch, Mr. Fontaine," I assured him, and left.

It had been a good-looking day when I arrived.

Now, it was positively handsome.

4

WHAT with stopping off for a hamburger and coffee on the way back into town, it was almost two o'clock when I reached the office. Candy Sullivan gave me one of her brilliant smiles.

"How did it go?"

I'd been thinking about what I was going to tell her about my latest assignment. My natural instinct was to be entirely open with her, stressing the confidential nature of the work, and generally stirring up her interest in what an important man I was, getting involved in all this top-level stuff. That was my natural instinct, or one of them. I have another, which carries with it a kind of over-drive, so that it assumes top-priority over any and all other emotions. This one I call self-preservation, and it has become

113

honed over the years to a very fine point.

The Sullivan might be a terrific attraction, was a terrific attraction, but she was also a total stranger. I knew nothing about how far she could be trusted, especially in the important area of my well-being. Don't misunderstand me, I'm not suggesting there was anything about her to give me cause for distrust. But there is trust and trust. If anyone outside got an inkling of what I was doing, I would be in trouble all round, and not least with my new client, J. J. Fontaine. For all his smooth ways and his general Ivy League background, I know a tough character when I see one, and I'd seen one that morning. I'd known Candy Sullivan for less than five hours, and most of that time had been spent out of the office. It wasn't the kind of well-cemented relationship which called for deep confidences.

I made sure that the door was firmly

114

shut behind me, and looked at her very seriously.

"You understand this is a very confidential business I have here?"

"Naturally," she replied, looking puzzled. "What about it?"

"You realise that anything you get to know while you're working here is more or less under a kind of oath of secrecy?" I insisted.

"Of course," and she was becoming rather flushed, "I have done quite a lot of extremely confidential work before, you know. I am not in the habit of going around prattling about my employer's business, no matter what kind it is. What are you leading up to, Mr. Preston?"

It hadn't been my intention to get her riled, and I hastened to sooth her down.

"Don't get upset," I urged, "but it's just that I had to make the point to you. This Fontaine thing comes under the general heading. As you said, he seems to be a man of some standing, and he certainly is upset about this bomb thing. I'm certainly glad I don't belong to this O.P.A."

"O.P.A?" she frowned. Evidently the term hadn't registered.

"The bomb-nuts," I explained, "the ones who call themselves the Oppressed Peoples of America. O.P.A. See?"

"Of course. Well, I can understand why you wouldn't want to be one of those crack-pots, but I don't see what that has to do with Mr. Fontaine."

She was about ready to buy the story now.

"Mr. Fontaine, if he gets his way, will personally butcher every member of the organisation. He told me exactly how he proposes to do it, and in loving detail. There is just the one small detail causing his a certain delay. He doesn't know where to find them."

"And so he hired you," she finished up for me. "He can't be serious, of course."

I looked affronted, sensing the answer to my next question.

"Why not?"

"What chance would you have?" she demanded. "One investigator, backed up by one female, with half a day's experience in the business. You have to concede that isn't a very impressive line-up, when you compare it with the F.B.I., plus the C.I.A., plus the State Police, the City Police, plus — "

"Whoa," I called. "Please plus me no more pluses. You are beginning to make the odds sound somewhat long."

"Long?" she scoffed, "I'd say they were out of sight."

Which was no more than the plain truth. I looked rueful, in a manly kind of way.

"Me too," I admitted. "I told him as much, but he wouldn't listen. He wants me to dig around anyway, and he's putting up five big ones for results. I won't get them, naturally, because as you say I have no chance against the other team. No, what'll happen is this. I have a minimum three-day fee, did I

117

mention that before?"

"No. What's the connection?"

"Just this. I'll be very surprised if the big-leaguers don't come up with something in that time, in which case I drop out. If they don't, then I'll simply tell him it's a no-hoper, collect three days pay, and quit the job."

Even when she was being serious, like now, her face was flawless.

"Isn't that being dishonest?" she asked.

"I don't think so. I shall roam around, ask a lot of questions, do what I can. The man is yelling for action, so I'll provide some. Who knows? I might even come up with something. I hope I do, I wouldn't mind getting a crack at the people who nearly bumped off Florence Digby."

Candy inspected me with eyes full of suspicion.

"All right, let us take this to it's unlikely extreme," and there was that doubt again, "let us suppose you do manage to get a line on these people, despite the odds. Will you really tell this man Fontaine? It sounds to me as though he'd charge them with a double-barreled shotgun or something. Is that really what you'd do?"

"Not exactly," I admitted. "Before I reported to Mr. Fontaine, I would first contact the proper authorities, tell them what I found out. Then, I'd take a few hours off, before reporting to my client. That would have given the big boys time to move in."

She snapped her fingers in triumph.

"There you are then. You are being dishonest. You are taking that man's money, with no intention of carrying out his wishes."

I made a show of trying another tack.

"Look at it this way," I entreated. "Mr. Fontaine wants to feel he's doing something. Something positive. I get elected for the job. I'm not going to cheat him. I'll do some work on it, but as you pointed out, I don't have a prayer against the opposition."

"I call taking five thousand dollars from a man, knowing you've already passed the information to the proper quarters, dishonest. I'd like to know what else you call it."

So that was what was bothering her. She really thought I would take the money.

"The five thousand? I'm not going to take that. You misunderstand me. What I'm taking is my three-day minimum, and nothing else. A job is a job, even if I know it's hopeless. And I have to eat."

It seemed to mollify her somewhat, but she still didn't like it.

"Well," she allowed grudgingly, "it's better than it first sounded, but I still don't think it's right."

"Look at it this way," I suggested. "J. J. Fontaine is determined to hire somebody, and with me he's lucky. I shall make a genuine effort to get some results. Believe me lady, there's plenty of people in this business who'd just sit on their butts, knowing it was hopeless, and send him a bill just the same. At least I'll be trying."

Something else occurred to her and she pointed a forefinger at me.

"Why doesn't he simply make an announcement? Why doesn't he tell everybody about this big reward? He'd have a much better chance that someone would come forward."

But I'd been expecting that one.

"He'd also have a much better chance of having a bomb tossed through his window," I reminded her. "These people are for real, and they are liable to get very annoyed with anybody who posts a reward on them. Don't forget they almost killed fifty people who didn't even know they existed, certainly wished them no harm. What would they do to a guy who was after their blood?"

The point was duly registered.

"Yes, I have to admit you're right there," she allowed. "All right, what do I do, open a file marked J. J. Fontaine, and start booking your time?"

Candy Sullivan might not know anything about the investigation business, but she was clearly familiar with the requirements of the Internal Revenue people. I didn't propose to bother those people with this little transaction. They have quite enough paper work as it is. On the other hand, I didn't intend to take the Sullivan into my confidence on that point. Let her open a file, all according to Hoyle. I could tear it up before Florence Digby came back.

"Yes, if you would," I nodded. "I'm going to have a quiet sit in the office, and try to decide where I start on this thing."

I left her there, happily working away on her short-lived file, and went to enjoy the peace and quiet of my own room. Lighting a cigaret, I pulled out the folded notes I had made at the Fontaine house, and began to study them.

Thanks to the rough, better make that crude, surgery on the original list, I had now only three names to contend with. The first thing I had to find out was whether any of them was still in the city. A planted bomb can cancel a flight, but it doesn't cancel out the intentions of the passengers. They had originally aimed for Boston and parts east, and presumably, having recovered from their little ordeal, they would by now have taken another flight. But Agent Witchley had given instructions that Florence Digby was to stick around for a few days. Was that because he still had some lingering doubts about her, or was it a general order for all the passengers of Flight 147?

Well, the only way to find out was to ask. I picked up the phone and asked Candy to get me the number the F.B.I., man had given me.

A man's voice replied, very cautious. "Who is that?"

"Name is Preston," I told him. "Agent Witchley told me I could get in touch with him at this number."

"He's not here right now. Mr. Preston, did you say? What's the

123

nature of your inquiry, Mr. Preston?"

I ignored that. One Witchley was bad enough. I didn't propose to involve the entire Bureau.

"What time will he be back?" I countered.

"Hard to say. I'll be glad to take a message for him."

"No message. Will you tell him I called, and I'll try again in one hour. If he wants to call me back, he has the number."

But he wasn't to be got rid of quite so easily.

"He may not have all his papers with him," he said easily. "Shall I just take a note of the number, just in case?"

I gave him the number, just in case, and hung up.

My three suspects did not make very promising reading. There were two men and one woman. Human nature being what it is, I took the woman first.

Her name was Diana Morrison, aged thirty-six, divorced, and she lived out at Settler's Valley, an expensive little development a few miles inland, and one which spoke well of her financial rating. She was some kind of chemist and had intended to attend a convention in Boston on this very day, Thursday. It was a one day seminar, and her return trip to Monkton City had already been reserved for Friday morning. As a prospective thief, I didn't rate her very highly. The people who had provided me via Fontaine with all those notes had been professionals. If they said she was a real chemist, then that's what she was. Not that I would count that a disqualification, standing by itself. The clincher for me was the conference. It was really pushing coincidence too hard altogether for a hundred other professionals to arrange a sudden conference, which would necessitate people flying in on the previous day, the very day chosen at random or force of circumstance by Walter M. Keane. These things are organised well ahead, months, and I almost decided not to bother with Dr. Morrison. There was only one reason I didn't cross her off the list, and that was because she hadn't made her reservation until so late in the day. It was still just a possibility that the conference was coincidental, and a convenient justification for the trip, which just happened to provide a first-class cover story for her.

I didn't have much hope about one of the men either, a certain Daniel P. Howe. This Howe was from Boston, where he was the local representative for a micro-chip manufacturing company based in Monkton City. It was part of his normal routine to attend a session every three months at the headquarters of the company. That had taken place on the Tuesday, which would make it logical that friend Howe would stay over, returning the following day. On the other hand, he could have taken an earlier flight. For some reason, he had chosen to wait until the late afternoon which was odd, but not sinister, in my book. He'd been staying at the Plaza Hotel on the Tuesday night, and my first move would have to be to find out whether he was still there. Here again, I thought the coincidence was too strong, that a quarterly gathering of company executives should just happen to take place at a time which made it convenient for their Boston representative to put in a little extra duty as a jewel-thief, on his way home. I would check it, as a matter of course, but I didn't like it.

My remaining male subject was a little more promising. Forty-one year old Michael Brooks was described as a general dealer, whatever that might be. He wasn't getting fat on the proceeds, that was for sure. His permanent address was listed as the Hotel Paradise on Twelfth Street, and I knew it well. Hotel it certainly was, but not exactly my idea of Paradise. It was about two levels up from the flophouse category, which would seem to suggest that the general dealing business was in a temporary recession period. Brooks had stated the reason for his trip east as being for purposes of business, nature unspecified. His reservation on Flight 147 had not been made until mid-day on Tuesday, so his business commitment would appear to have come about quite suddenly. Yes, there was no doubt that of the three, I liked Mr. Brooks a whole lot better than the other candidates.

It wasn't really any of my business, and it was doubtful whether it had any connection with my investigation, but I wondered why these people had not received the accolade from the security clearance brigade. There was nothing in any of their notes to suggest any subversive links. Well, I wasn't going to bother my head about it. Other people would be working on that angle, I had no doubt, and they would be far better qualified. Besides which, that wasn't what I was getting paid for. My job was to find somebody who could use an extra quarter of a million dollars, and who wasn't particular about how they acquired it. The first half of that particular equation would embrace just about the entire population, but it was the second half which was the clincher.

Doctor Morrison I saved for last. Having presumably missed out on the Boston conference, she was probably back at her normal job at that hour of the day. My first call was to the Plaza Hotel, where I was told that Daniel P. Howe had extended his stay, and was intending to remain in the city at least one more night. No, they could not put me through to his room, because instructions had been left that he was not to be disturbed. I didn't bother to ask why. Even if they knew, they wouldn't tell me.

There was no point in phoning the Paradise. It wasn't the kind of place with a regular reception area. There were no conference delegates to be booked in, no banquets to arrange, in fact not much of anything at all by the way of service. There would be a counter, a register, and an old man looking after the whole shebang. Either that, or a kid fresh out of school. Anyone who came cheap would be able to cope with the reception facilities at the Hotel Paradise. I heaved up out of the chair and knew I'd have to brave the afternoon heat outside.

Candy Sullivan looked at me with eyes full of questions.

"I'm going out," I informed her, "start sniffing around."

"Will I be able to contact you?"

"No, I'm afraid you won't. If I don't make it back here by five o'clock, would you just be sure the door is locked when you leave?"

"So I may not see you again today?"

It could mean something, or nothing. Was she perhaps wondering about some time later than five o'clock? Say around dinner-time for instance? It was a pleasant thought, but I would have to be firm with myself. My time was not really my own, and especially the evenings. That is the time when the rats come out of their holes, and if I was in business as a rat-catcher, then I wouldn't have any time for dalliance.

"Probably not," I replied, hoping the reluctance in my tone would register. "If not, I'll see you in the morning, right?"

"I'll be here," she promised. "Nine sharp."

The heat was as bad as I'd feared, and my clothes were sticking to me by the time I reached the Hotel Paradise. Like I said before, it's neither one thing nor the other. By no means a flophouse on the one hand, and equally no place for a special presentation of our newest product, gentlemen. The reception desk was the last word in cheap plastic, and the clerk was a surly looking youth who might have passed for seventeen in the half-dark.

"You want a room?" he asked, without enthusiasm.

"Just calling on a friend," I told him nicely. "Only I forget his room-number.

Name of Brooks, Mr. Brooks."

"Brooks," he repeated, "Brooks," as though trying to remember something.

"Try the register," I suggested.

He looked at the heavy book on the counter, shrugged, and began thumbing over the leaves. By the time he'd reached the third page back, the effort was beginning to exhaust him.

"Doesn't seem to be no Brooks," he offered.

"There has to be," I told him firmly. "The man lives here."

"Oh, a permanent." That seemed to explain everything. "Why'nt you say so? We got a separate list for those guys."

Turning now to the very last pages, he ran a dirty finger down a list. The finger stopped, and he looked up in triumph.

"Sure, here he is. One O Seven. Got his own bath and everything."

"Imagine."

I walked up two flights of worn carpet, and down a corridor until

I located the room number. Then I tapped lightly on the door. Some shuffling from the other side, than a man's voice.

"Who is it?"

"Laundry, Mr. Brooks."

A chain slid back, then the door opened.

"That's pretty quick. I only — hey, you ain't no laundry man."

But he wasn't alarmed, only puzzled. He was shortish, with a roly-poly build under the Hawaiian shirt, and had the general air of a man who'd spent too much time at the cream doughnuts counter. Soft, flabby, and of a nervous disposition if the darting eyes and furtive expression were any indication.

"Just like a few words, Mr. Brooks."

I pushed past him into the room, and he made no move to stop me. The feeling that I was wasting my time was already strong in me, and I had no wish to prolong our interview more than necessary. Mr. Brooks was not a neat liver. The bed was rumpled, there were clothes dropped around on chairs, some on the floor, and a pile of girlie magazines rested on the bedside table. A box of chocolates lay open at the foot of the bed, and most of the contents were just waxed paper memories. The air was foul with the smoke of cheap cigarets, plus the extra odour of the proud occupant. The kid downstairs had said he had his own bathroom. The atmosphere said he should spend more time in it.

"You another cop?" he demanded, but there was more pleading than force behind the words.

I stared into the pudgy, anxious face.

"Now, why should I be a cop?" I countered.

"I don't know," he confessed, shrugging. "I've seen so many of those guys the past twenty four hours, another one here or there don't make no difference."

"Really? And what did they want from you?"

"Well," he began, then pulled himself together. "Now, wait just a minute here. This is my place, and you got no right to come busting in here without a warrant. That's the law."

"So it is," I agreed, smiling without friendliness. "But I don't happen to be a police officer, Mr. Brooks, so I don't have to concern myself with those details. All I want from you is a few answers, and I'll be on my way."

"Zasso?" Something approaching confidence was now building up inside him. "Now, I tell you what you do. You just walk straight out of here, or I'm going to shout for some law."

I didn't want to hurt him, but I also hadn't any inclination to stay in that foul atmosphere longer than was absolutely necessary. Keeping the first two fingers of my right hand very stiff, I poked them sharply into him where his belly was hidden. A great whoosh of breath emptied from him, making me turn my head aside, and he sat down with a bump on the bed. Alarm was now large on his face.

"What is this, some kind of shakedown?" he whispered. "Listen, there ain't twenty bucks in the whole place."

"Just tell me two things and I'll go. You keep the twenty."

That restored him a little. Not much, but a little.

"What kinda things?"

"First, why did you book a flight to Boston?"

"Is that all?" and he seemed relieved. "Nothing funny about that. I had to see a guy."

"What guy?"

"Little business matter. I'm a dealer, you see. I heard this guy had something over there, and I got a customer for it. Coulda made a couple of hundred, clear," he added dolefully.

"There are three flights a day to Boston," I pointed out. "Why are you still here?"

He looked puzzled by the question.

"Because of the cops is why. They

kept me over there half the night, going on about this and that. I mean, I'm as good a citizen as the next guy, and I don't mind doing my duty, but I say they didn't have no right. Now, because of those guys, I lost my chance at this piece, and the two hundred that went with it. I'm going to sue the United States Government, and I told them so. I got a good lawyer, real sharp."

He was so aggrieved, and full of righteous indignation that I couldn't resist another smile, but this time with some humour in it.

"You really told 'em, eh?"

"Betcha. You can push a man just so far, I don't care how many badges you got, then he comes back at you. Well, I'm going to go for Uncle Sam, and I'm going to win, too. What's all this got to do with you?"

"Never mind," I was wasting my time with this outraged slob, and time was a precious commodity on this job. "Good luck with your case, Mr.

Brooks. I don't think we'll be meeting again."

When I reached the door, thankful for the air coming in from the corridor, he called.

"Hey. I thought you said two questions."

I looked back at him, still sitting there next to the remnants of the chocolate box.

"You already answered both of them."

"You still didn't tell me who you was," he pointed out.

"It doesn't matter. I don't think we'll meet again. Good luck with your lawsuit."

Back in the car, I crossed out Michael Brooks very firmly. He'd been my best shot, or so I'd thought originally, and I was not very hopeful about the others. It was still to early for Dr. Diana Morrison to have finished her day's work, assuming that she'd reported for duty, so I went around to the Plaza Hotel, to take a look at the other man,

Daniel P. Howe. There was a row of pay-phones in a rear lobby, and I put in a call.

"Plaza Hotel," said a pleasant female voice.

"Post Office," I announced crisply. "We have a special delivery for Mr. Daniel P. Howe, but the address is only given as the Plaza Hotel. There are several, as you probably know, and I'm trying them all. Could you check your register, please?"

"Just hold on." She didn't keep me long, before she was back with her triumphant announcement. "Yes, we have Mr. Howe."

"That is Daniel P?" I pressed.

"It is indeed."

"Thank you very much," I said, sounding relieved. "What room number shall I put on this?"

"Five One Nine," she informed me.

"Thank you for your co-operation, I'll have this delivered within the hour."

Cradling the phone, I made my way

to the elevators. One good thing, from my point of view, about places like the Plaza, is that you can wander in and out more or less at random. Nobody bothers to ask who you are or what you want, so long as you do nothing to attract attention. I took myself up to Five, stepped out onto thick carpet which was a far cry from the Paradise, and followed the pointing arrows until I reached 519. True enough, there was a notice on the door. Do Not Disturb. I rapped on the door, which was soon opened by a gray-haired severe-looking man in a formal business suit, despite the heat.

"What is the meaning of this?" he demanded. "Didn't you see the notice?"

"This won't take a minute," I assured him. "Sorry if I disturbed you, Mr. Howe."

His glare intensified.

"I am not Mr. Howe," he snapped. "I am Doctor Elkin, and I am here to attend Mr. Howe. Who the devil might you be?"

Doctor Elkin was nobody's Michael Brooks. I wouldn't get away with pushing past him. Approach Number Three was required, the mask of officialdom. When I spoke, it was the calm authority.

"Deputy Sheriff Preston," I informed him. "I am making contact with all passengers who were involved in the bomb attempt yesterday afternoon. Would it be possible for me to see Mr. Howe? I'll be as quick as I can."

He looked at me coldly, and I waited for him to call me on that Deputy Sheriff bid. It's perfectly true that I have that title, and even a card that says so. There was one time I was of some service to a bunch of the local big-wigs from some out-of-state convention. I spent most of the night with them after that, swapping drinks and lies, and at the end of it all, they awarded me the honorary title. The only weakness about it is that it's honorary, in the first place, and even that carries no weight in my city, because these characters were from Mudville, Nebraska or Bogtown, Kansas or someplace.

"I'm sorry officer," he decided, "it's out of the question. Mr. Howe is under sedation, and won't regain consciousness for quite some time. Perhaps I could help you. What was it you wanted to ask him? Two other people have already been here, and I should have thought that was enough."

I thought quickly.

"Mine is what you might call a follow-up," I explained, "but if Mr. Howe is under sedation, I guess I have my answer. You see, I was going to ask whether he had received any telephone threats, or messages from this terrorist organisation."

He seemed to like it, and even went so far as to give me a reply.

"As to that," he returned, "the answer is a categoric 'no'. But then, I couldn't say whether anyone has attempted a telephone call. It would have been blocked by the people at the desk."

"Of course," I understood, "tell me, doctor, what's the nature of Mr. Howe's illness?"

"Didn't your colleagues tell you that?" he queried. "Or is this one of those situations where half a dozen agencies are involved, and nobody shares with anyone else?"

Dr. Elkin was nobody's fool, that much was clear.

"By no means," I assured him. "Co-operation between us all is total in this kind of situation. But you must appreciate we are all under a great deal of pressure, and there just isn't time for sitting around tables, swapping notes."

"Yes, yes, I can understand that. Mr. Howe was one of those who received an emergency shot during the evacuation of the aircraft. He's a highly strung individual, and I'm afraid he rather panicked at the time. That made him a threat to the safety of other passengers, and the medical team are equipped to deal with precisely that situation, as you must know. And, of course, I attach no blame to them. There is no time for refinements in an emergency of that nature. The greatest good of the greatest number has to be priority one."

I knew that what he said was true. The medics would have been on hand with their needles, as a matter of routine. At the first sign of any hold-up resulting from somebody losing his head, in went the plunger. But the effect is short-lived, and the incident was now twenty-four hours old. Howe should have been out of it long hours since.

"I've never know effects to last this long," I said, and there was a tinge of surprise in the words.

Elkin shook his head.

"Not in the ordinary way. The effects usually wear off after thirty minutes or so, but Mr. Howe is not an ordinary case. He has a very rare blood ailment, which does not affect his life, so long as he obeys with a few basic rules. His reaction to the injection was a disaster, or almost, and it was lucky for him he carries with him a card which tells anyone with the slightest medical knowledge that he needs immediate treatment. The airport team realised at once what had happened, and he was in a hospital within the hour. Most efficient, most."

So that meant that Daniel P. Howe could be pencilled out. He had been under constant medical supervision of one kind or another, ever since he came off Flight 147, and in bad physical shape. I thanked the doctor and left.

Downstairs, I paused at the row of pay-phones, wondering. There was a call to be made, but maybe it would be better if I put some distance between me and the Plaza Hotel. Dr. Elkin had set me wondering, and the sooner I cleared my mind the better. Since I was only a couple of blocks from the railroad terminal, I drove around there, hoping to find at least one phone that hadn't been vandalised, or the mechanism jammed with lead dimes. When I finally located one, I called the airport, and asked for the Emergency Medical Unit. The phone was picked up at once.

"E.M.U." announced a crisp voice.

"Mr. Travis, this is the Monkton City Globe," I told him importantly. "We hear that one of the passengers rescued from the Boston plane yesterday has had a very bad reaction to the sedative which was injected into him. Mr. Daniel P. Howe, of the Plaza Hotel."

There was silence at the other end, and it was clear my call was not the most welcome they'd had that day.

"The Monkton City Globe, you say?"

"That's it," I confirmed. "The way we hear it, your people used the wrong stuff, and this man Howe nearly died. We're naturally very concerned, and our readers are entitled — "

"Just a moment," he cut in. "You

have this all wrong. Mr. Howe happens to be a very special case. Are you the medical correspondent?"

"General features," I replied, "I'm just running the initial story, and we go to press in forty minutes. Our own doctors will give a far more thorough coverage when they've had more time to look into it."

Now he was definitely alarmed.

"Look, this is a very serious matter," he said urgently. "You could give the public an entirely wrong impression here. We have used the same preparation many hundreds of times in the past, and there had never been the slightest — "

"Mr. Travis," I cut in, sounding weary. "We are not living in the past. We are talking about a possible medical error in the Flight 147 evacuation. Perfectly understandable, in all the panic, but you must appreciate — "

" — panic?", he interjected. "There's no question of any panic. This unit is ready at all times for precisely such a situation. And let me point out that

Mr. Howe was the only one with a bad reaction."

I grinned happily. We were getting down to the meat.

"The only one? You mean there were other people who received the same treatment, and suffered no ill-effects? Is that what you're saying?"

"Precisely," snapped Travis, "and if you will let me talk to someone with medical knowledge, I can quickly clear his mind."

"Not up to me. Editor's decision," I replied. "Tell you what I can do. I'll check on these other people, right now, before I put the item on the editor's desk. It's in your own interests, you must see that. If the others are O.K., it could make the difference. Do you have their names?"

He did some more thinking.

"I don't know about this," he stalled, "It's all most irregular."

"So is killing of passengers," I told him savagely. "O.K. I'll go ahead without you. Air Passenger Nears

148

Death, Authorities Refuse Comment. Something like that. Page One, no doubt about it. Could I have your first name, Mr. Travis?"

"No, wait a minute," The unfortunate Travis was probably wishing he'd taken that late vacation after all. "There were only two others involved. I can't see any real harm in telling you their names. You'd get them in the end, anyway. Matter of record."

"You bet it is," I emphasised. "My promise still holds. Just give me the names, and they'll be checked out right now."

"Just a minute, while I get the file."

With my hand over the mouthpiece I did a happy little whistle, to the annoyance of a fierce-looking lady who was waiting her turn with the phone. I winked at her, and she looked even more ferocious than before. Travis came back on the line.

"There were two other emergency injections," he announced. "A Mrs.

Annie Kowalski — " he went on with the home address, but I was paying no attention " — and the other was a man named Keane. Walter M. Keane. He lives at — "

I also knew where he lived at, and that he was not available, but I didn't bother Travis with my knowledge. Now that I had what I wanted, I gave him all kinds of assurances, and hung up.

Walter M. Keane. It seemed too good to be true.

There must have been an odd expression on my face, because the waiting woman took a distinct step backwards as I passed.

Keane had been one of the people who seemed to be holding up the evacuation of the airplane, or so the medics thought. But he was still feeling the effects of his nerve-calming tablet at the time. That made his version of what happened immediately suspect. He'd been jostled he said, and maybe he had, but not necessarily by the thief. All he knew was that when he came to himself, the stones were gone, and his last recollection was of someone barging into him at the head of the chute. It was natural he would put the two things together. Natural, but not necessarily correct. It could be that he just happened to get pushed by another passenger, who was himself losing control, and went bucketing down the inflated plastic, apparently in a panic, to be promptly injected and got out of the way, in the emergency routine procedure. Dr. Elkin had told me the effects would normally wear off in half an hour or so. Keane would probably attribute his passing out to the drug he had himself administered. It was possible he didn't even realise he'd been injected.

Then another thought struck me.

It was equally possible that he knew about it, but kept it from the people he was working with, in case they marked him unreliable. As J. J. Fontaine had been at pains to make clear, the precious stone trade operated largely on personal trust. At a quarter of a million dollars per throw, who could afford to trust a man liable to lose his head?

Although I couldn't find much fault with my reasoning, it didn't make me very happy with the kind of conclusion it led to. Because, if that brief-case had not been taken by someone on the airplane, which I'd been assuming from the start, then we had a whole new ballgame. If the case had been in Keane's possession when he made his flailing exit, then it went missing at some later time. Instead of being able to concentrate on the comparatively small list of passengers, I would now have to take into account a small army of people. Rescue crews, firemen, medics, police, and anybody else who had a reason to rush out to the site of the emergency. Anyone of those people could be the one I was looking for, and the thought did little to cheer me up.

As I walked slowly away from the phone-booth, I caught sight of the departure board. Other people would shortly be leaving for San Francisco and points northward. Or they, could go the other way and head for San Diego and on to the delights of Baja California. I had a sudden impulse to go to the ticket windows and take a train out, direction immaterial. It was a ridiculous idea, and I dismissed it at once.

Maybe it would have been better if I'd gone.

5

MONKTON CITY Airport is a small affair, and in no way would it bear any comparison with its neighbouring giant at Los Angeles, for which it frequently acts as a relief unit at especially busy times. Most of the big airlines keep up a token appearance, but little more. The air traffic is small but steady, and it is a favorite with the private owners, who are glad to be able to avoid the hassle of clearance which is inevitable at the large fields. The security chief is Myron Filby, a grizzled ex-F.B.I., man, with whom I had had dealings in the past. On the whole, we hit it off pretty well, but he is not a man to fool with. He takes as much jealous care of his airport, and the reputations of its various users, as he used to lavish on the safety of certain Presidents in his younger days. Now turned fifty, he had kept his five feet ten and his hundred and eighty pounds in good fighting trim, and taking him all round, he was a man I preferred to have on the same side as me.

He was seated at his desk studying papers when an assistant showed me in. Rising, he stuck out a hand and gave me a quizzical grin.

"Wondered if you'd show up," he grunted.

"Oh? What made you think I might?"

"Several things." He waved a hand towards a chair and I sat down. He did the same, looking across at me with eyes that had seen many things. "For one thing, the passenger list. Lady on it by the name of Digby. I was very interested to note her occupation."

"Might have known you wouldn't miss that," I acknowledged. "And for another thing?"

The deep eyes twinkled.

"For another thing, a little bird

mentioned your name."

I might have known. These F.B.I., people stick together like brothers, and that 'ex' tag doesn't mean a thing.

"That would be the ring-necked Witchley bird, easily distinguished by it's very close plumage," I supposed.

"Maybe. Anyway, you're here. Why?"

"Probably wasting my time," I admitted, "but not yours, I think."

Thick spatulate fingers spread out on the table in front of him.

"That has to come under the general classification of cryptic remarks," he observed drily. "Can't recall when I heard a cryptier. What does it mean? In English, please."

"You understand, Chief Filby," I had already decided this was to be one of those 'chief' situations, "that I cannot be compelled to reveal the identity of my client? That is a matter of simple law."

"Under the terms of your license, which is granted by this State, that is the simple law," he replied gently.

"What is in progress here is a matter for federal jurisdiction, involving a whole set of laws which are not nearly so simple. Unkind people have been heard to say that the Federals make their own laws. I am not one of those people, and indeed I refute the suggestion. Nevertheless, I advise you to tread with caution, and not to try hiding behind your license too much. It is a very small document to cover someone as big as you."

It was a fair warning, and one that I intended to pay every regard. All the same, I thought the story I had concocted was probably good enough to keep me out of harm's way. I certainly hoped so.

"My enquiries are not directed at this terrorist business," I assured him. "It's true that the bomb affair is what caused me to be hired, but really the circumstances of the case are only coincidental."

I wanted to get that area cleared at the outset. Filby nodded.

"I'll decide what I think about that when I've heard the rest of it," he told me, guardedly. "Could we get to the point now?"

"I'm interested in the emergency services," I announced. "More especially, I am looking into the medical unit, which caused the near-death of David P. Howe, one of the passengers on Flight 147, by the injection of an unsafe serum."

If I was expecting a dramatic reaction, I was to be disappointed. This man opposite had been on the wrong end of bombs, guns and knives most of his adult life. A few words were unlikely to worry him too much.

"That's quite a statement," he replied, without emotion. "Unsafe serum, I think you said. Have you anything to back that up?"

"It almost killed Mr. Howe," I pointed out. "If that doesn't qualify it as unsafe, I don't know what does."

"Has anybody told you that Mr. Howe is a most unusual man, in the medical sense? That he has some rare blood problem, with the result that he reacted badly to the serum, which is used throughout this country probably a hundred thousand times a day? Every day," he emphasised.

The chief had lead me to my major point without prompting, which was a bonus.

"Exactly," I agreed. "The serum, as you correctly say, is in daily use across the country in hospitals, airports, railroad stations, any place that carries any medical facility. The manufacture and supply of that stuff is big business, and competition is fierce among the large chemical companies. If it should be that the serum supplied by the present manufacturer is in any way less foolproof than something which can be offered by another source, contracts worth millions would be channeled in a different direction. I think you begin to see what I'm driving at?"

He moved his head sideways, in part-denial.

"Not sure yet. When you started off, I thought you were representing Mr. Howe himself, or perhaps his family, his employers. Someone who might think they have a case for a lawsuit against the airline. Or this airport. Or both. But the way you're putting it makes me do a re-think on that. You're after bigger fish, by the sound of it, and that's where it starts to come apart."

It was a fortunate thing for me that I had gone into that office with a well-thought-out story. I thought I knew what was coming next, but it would be better if he made his own points.

"Now, you're losing me," I admitted. "Come apart in what way?"

"This way." He leaned back in the swivel chair, and swung sideways to me, but could still watch my face out of the corner of his eye. "Let us take a purely hypothetical situation. Let us take a case where some big financial interest thinks this Howe thing is worth looking into. I am talking here of a chemical combine of some kind, a big operation. They want to mount an enquiry, get boards of officials involved, quite possibly begin pulling gently on a few political strings. How would they set about it? I can think, offhand, of three different approaches at least. All of them involve medical men and/or highly qualified chemists at the very minimum. Don't take this next as an offensive remark because I don't intend it to be. The very last thing they would do would be to entrust a matter of that scale to a one-man organisation like yours."

He stopped, as if surprised by the vigor with which I was wagging my head in assent.

"You are absolutely right, Chief. Dead on the button. We're still talking about a hypothesis, by the way, are we not?"

"Yup." The eye facing me was taking in every line of my features.

"As you say, this imaginary combine would certainly not need anyone like me to start off something big. I might well make the same point to them myself, if I were even approached. But let us look a little further into the particular instance which raised all this. Might not such people want to proceed with a great deal of care, before investing hundreds of thousands of dollars in some campaign which might prove to be a waste of time?"

It's very unnerving addressing only one eye, particularly when it doesn't even blink.

"I'm still listening" he assured me.

"Wouldn't it be more practical to find out the precise details, at a cost of only a few hundred dollars, before going any further? For a job like that, we're at the other extreme of the scale. And that," pointing a modest finger at my chest, "is where someone like me would come in."

He thought about if for a few moments then swung himself back towards me again.

"What kind of precise details?"

"Such as who gave Mr. Howe his shot, for one thing? Was he a new man, inexperienced? Where is the serum stored, for another? How does the operative concerned keep his equipment sterile? Is there any possibility of any extraneous matter getting into Howe's bloodstream along with the serum? In short, Chief can this be put down to a question of simple incompetence, or unprofessional behaviour, in this one isolated instance? I'm no chemist or doctor, but I know a lot about asking questions, and I ought to be able to pinpoint a situation of that kind. Or," I added quickly, "if I felt there was one particular area where medical knowledge would be needed in order to make a judgement, then I could say that too."

He didn't like it too well, but he preferred it to his earlier thinking.

"Of course, I could just tell you to get the hell out of my airport," he reminded. "What would you do then?"

"I would go, and fast," I returned. "I would simply report that the authorities had clamped down, send in my bill, and forget it. Whether my clients would be happy with that situation, whether they would be prepared to let things rest like that, I leave it for you to judge."

By late afternoon, his beard was beginning to lose it's morning freshness. There was a rasping sound as he pulled a heavy thumb along his jaw.

"The way it stacks up is this," he growled ruminatively, "either I turn you loose on the airport medics, or you go away and a whole bunch of heavies moves in from God-knows where. I don't think I care for the alternative. Let's say I give you a shot at it, how do I know I can trust you?"

"Trust me, in what way?"

"Put it this way," he suggested. "Let's assume you do find something. I think it's unlikely, but let's assume. That would let your clients out, if

I understand what you've just been telling me?"

"As I see it, yes. It would simply be a local affair, and they would lose interest at once. I'd pick up my pay, and go to the racetrack."

"Ah, but that's just it," he sighed. "Would you?"

He'd lost me again, and I said so.

"You lost me."

"Suppose it turns out to be what you call a local matter, and the interest of these hypothetical clients fades away. Some people might think to themselves, well, well, what have we here? A nice lawsuit for somebody else to pick up. The man Howe for one, and all those others we talked about earlier. What's to prevent you from going straight to them, with good solid information gained with the approval of no less a person than the Chief Security Officer of the complex? Well?"

My affronted look was getting plenty of exercise today.

"You don't know me too well, Chief Filby," I said huffily, "but that is not the way I behave. People who trust me don't live to regret it. I'm here for one purpose only, and if you help me to achieve that purpose, the matter ends there so far as I'm concerned. Don't take my word for it. Call downtown. Ask the people at police headquarters whether my word is any good. They may not love me down there, but they'll give me that."

"All right, I will. Who do I ask for?" He reached for a telephone.

"Rourke of Homicide. Or Randall. Matthews of Burglary, almost anybody. Pick a name. It really won't matter."

He already had the receiver in his hand, but now he put it back in it's cradle.

"Good enough. I'll believe you. How do I explain you to the people here? Do you work for any of the insurance companies?"

"Most of the big ones. On and off. Nothing regular."

166

"Tell me you're an insurance investigator."

Deadpan, he asked me. Deadpan I replied.

"I'm an insurance investigator."

"O.K. Come on."

Ten minutes later, after we had threaded our way through the quiet bustle of the public areas, he led me to a door with 'E.M.U.' stencilled clear. A brief tap, and he opened it, walking inside. Two men sat at a small table by the grilled window, playing cards. A third man reclined in a low chair, working his way through a hefty paperback novel.

"Afternoon," greeted Chief Filby. "Sorry to disturb you but this is Mr. Preston. He's an insurance investigator, and he'd like to ask you some questions."

The card-players groaned, while the reader simply looked resigned.

"More questions?" One of the players put his cards down, face to the table, and stared at me.

"I'm afraid so, Doc." Turning to me, my escort said. "This is Doctor Eric Tripp. He's in charge here. I'll leave you to it. We'll have another word before you leave, huh?"

I can recognise an order when I hear one.

"Of course."

He went out. Dr. Tripp came over to me, holding out his hand. The others watched.

"Don't mind us, Mr. Preston. We got just a little bit up to here with questions last night."

"Night," snorted the reading man. "They kept us here till almost three a.m."

"I'll be as little trouble as I can," I assured them all. "This won't take too long. Can we talk somewhere, Dr. Tripp?"

There were no spare chairs in the room. He nodded to a door at the side, and we went through into another, lighter room where three army type cots were neatly laid out. Tripp parked himself on one of those, and I sat on another, facing him.

"Technically," he explained, "this is our waiting room for emergency patients while we're waiting for them to be taken away. On the more practical side, we take it in turns to sack out during night shifts. No point in three men listening out for one bell."

He was young, not yet thirty, and easy to talk with. As he began to answer my questions, I was able to sketch in the skeleton of the administration of the system. All the emergency services worked a three-shift twenty-four hour system. Midnight till eight a.m., eight till four, four to midnight. It was almost four-twenty, so I was talking to the same people who'd been on duty for the bomb incident.

"So, you'd only just started your shift when the emergency call came yesterday?"

"Damn right," he grumbled. "Twenty minutes earlier, and the day crowd would have caught it. Mind you, I'm glad I didn't miss it, in a way. My first bomb, you know? I've often wondered how I would react in a live situation. I mean, I've done a thousand drills, but that is no substitute for the real thing. Actually being out there, and trying to do your work knowing a bomb might go off any minute, that's a very different experience. And yet, the funny thing was, once you get into that live situation, with real people, you work automatically. You don't even think about why you're there. Very strange feeling."

I nodded, and said complimentary things about the performance, then led him back to details. Each shift consisted of one doctor and two paramedics. One of the paras drove the ambulance, with the doctor up front, and the second para in back. The ambulance was fitted out with the usual emergency life-saving apparatus, but each man carried his own kit, and was personally responsible for the contents, which were inspected at intervals. I said I would like to have a look at those myself, and then explained my presence, as being a precautionary move against possible future action by some party or parties unknown.

"It was probably your quick thinking that saved Passenger Howe's life, doctor. How quickly did you recognise that he was reacting badly to the serum?"

"Almost at once, and it didn't need much quick thinking. His reaction was immediate and massive. We were able to get him into the ambulance within seconds, and carry out counter measures."

"We?"

"Two-man job, hauling a dead weight," he explained. "Oh that's not a very good choice of phrase, is it? Make that live weight."

We grinned at the small joke.

"Mr. Howe was only one of three people who received shots," I went on, "the others were a Mrs. Kowalski, and a Mr. Keane. Did you handle those yourself as well?"

"No, not both. I attended to Mrs. Kowalski, but Jack Griswold dealt with Mr. Keane. There's no question about rank involved here, Mr. Preston. These men are well-qualified to administer those injections, otherwise they wouldn't be here. What happens is, one man stands either side of the chute, the third man at the bottom. At the first sign of any behaviour on the part of a passenger, which could cause delay, we don't hesitate. In goes the needle. Don't make the common error of thinking that is unfeeling. It's just that there isn't time for any pleading or cajoling, which we would do under normal circumstances. Our job is to see that everybody gets off that aircraft and away. And don't forget that time is being measured in seconds, not minutes."

I felt awkward, having this man justifying himself to me. He had nothing to apologise for, quite the reverse. The whole team, indeed all the emergency people, had done a fine job the previous day, and they ought to be getting medals, not questions. What I really wanted was to talk with Jack Griswold, but I would have to make my way through the elaborate pretense which was my justification for being there.

"I fully understand," I assured him, "and believe me, there is no question of anyone being criticised here. On the contrary, my business is to make it plain that everything and everyone here is beyond criticism, which, off the record, happens to coincide with my own opinion."

He liked that, and smiled.

"Last night, by the time some of those people got through with their question, I was beginning to wonder whether any of us had done a single thing that was right. It was like being dissected."

"I can imagine," I soothed. "So there was you and Griswold, and could I have the name of the third member of your team?"

"Halloran," he replied promptly. "That was him, glaring at you for interrupting his reading."

So the other card-player was my man.

"I wouldn't have thought that was as serious as breaking up a card-game," I contributed. "Who was winning, you or Griswold?"

He stared at me for a second, nonplussed. Then his face cleared.

"Oh, I see. Yes, of course. You're naturally assuming my opponent was Griswold. No, no, that's our regular man, Don Lawrence. And he won't mind a bit. He was already in to me for five thousand when you arrived. We play a hundred dollars a point, you see, just to keep our debts within reasonable limits."

Another joke, and I contrived a thin smile, although I wasn't really paying attention. My thoughts were elsewhere. Everywhere. In the room next door the public address system crackled suddenly, and details of departures came over in clear tones. Dr. Tripp cocked an ear to the voice, while waiting for me to say something.

"So Lawrence wasn't on duty at the time of the incident? Was it his day off or something?"

"No. He called in earlier to warn us he wouldn't show. Some kind of stomach upset. He's alright now."

"Good, good," I enthused, "it's a lucky thing Griswold was available." My doctor friend didn't like that.

"Lucky? There's no luck about it. The system is pre-planned to take care of any such situation. No, all that happens is, one of us has to do a double-shift. We don't like it, as you can imagine, but it doesn't happen very often. Mind you, if Griswold had known what was coming, he wouldn't have been so quick to volunteer. That man started work at eight yesterday morning, and didn't get away until the rest of us did, at three o'clock this morning. That is nineteen hours of consecutive duty, and that is too much in anybody's book."

"Right," I agreed. "But he couldn't have been fit for work again by eight this morning, surely?"

"Oh, no," he assented. "One of the night guys stayed on while Jack caught up with his sleep. He was out on his feet when he left here this morning. Even forgot his bag."

"His bag?"

The back of my neck was beginning to make little bristlings, which happens sometimes when I'm getting close to something good.

"His kit," explained Dr. Tripp. "We usually guard those things like they were our own children. Yes, that was one tired man. New bag, too, he was quite proud of it. He'd been showing it to us before the balloon went up."

I looked at my watch. It was a few minutes before five, and Candy Sullivan would be locking up the store. I remembered that I hadn't yet had my reply from Agent Witchley.

"Excuse me, doctor, but is there a telephone I could use? I ought to call my office before everybody goes home."

"Oh certainly. You'll have to step outside I'm afraid. No one, but no one is permitted to use the phone in here except for medical matters. We're supposed to be an emergency unit, you know."

I went out into the corridor, and walked the twenty yards to the phone, stuck in my plastic and called the office.

"Preston Investigations," announced the voice I was coming to know. "Can I help you?"

"There's no answer to that," I told her. "This is Preston. Just wondered if anything came up while I've been out."

"Oh yes, there is one message," she replied. "A Mr. Witchley? Said he was returning your call, and you would know where to find him. Is everything

177

going well, Mr. Preston?"

"I'm not getting much by the way of results," I hedged. "I won't get back now, so I'll see you tomorrow, Candy."

She didn't answer at once, but I was quite willing to wait.

"I was just thinking," she said casually. "If you suddenly realised you had some special instructions for me tomorrow, you wouldn't know how to contact me. Had I better give you my home number?"

That was one of those offers you usually only dream about. Keeping my tone as casual as hers, I hoped, I fell in with the idea.

"Probably just as well, let me find a pen."

I copied down the number with loving care, thanked her, and we told each other goodbye. Well, I congratulated myself, we both went through that little charade very neatly, and now I had to get back to what I was being paid to do.

Doctor Tripp was in the outer room again, talking with the others. The way they all stopped when I returned made the subject of the conversation easy to guess. They were all standing together in the middle of the room, Halloran's book lying unheeded by the chair. I spoke to the third man, Lawrence.

"Dr. Tripp tells me you've been sick, Mr. Halloran. Fully recovered now, I trust?"

"Yeah," he replied with a shame-faced grin. "Damndest thing hit me in the gut, but it went as fast as it came. Some twenty-four hour bug, I guess."

"That's what it must have been."

It would have created suspicion if I'd pushed him on the point. After all, his stomach troubles were none of my concern, and I was supposed only to be interested in something that had happened when he hadn't been on duty. But I would have laid a small wager that Lawrence's bug hadn't arrived out of the atmosphere.

For my money, he had somehow been slipped a little something which would keep him out of the way. I didn't want to waste any more time than was absolutely necessary with the rest of the team. The man I wanted to see was this Griswold, but I knew I had to put some kind of a showing in the unit before I could break away.

"Well now doctor," I said heartily, "the sooner I get on with my little investigation, the sooner you'll be rid of me."

I spent the next hour poking around, asking all kinds of pointless questions and making notes. I studied the interior of the ambulance, checked the medical stores, included the refrigerated plasma and serum. I looked at Dr. Tripp's personal bag, and also Halloran's. They demonstrated with some pride the orderly fashion in which everything was laid out, sterilised and ready, then locked them carefully afterwards. They also pulled my leg gently a couple of times, with medical gags they knew I couldn't follow. Everything was orderly and immaculate, and it hadn't been done for my benefit. Nobody expected me. What I was seeing was a hyper-efficient unit, ready to move.

In one corner of the room stood a black leather briefcase, shining new.

"That must be Griswold's kit, I imagine?" I queried, pointing.

"That's it," confirmed Halloran. "Old Jack must have been really beat to go leaving that behind. He just bought it this week."

"Won't he worry about it?" I asked. "I mean, supposing one of you ran out of hypodermics or something?"

Some of the good humour went out of their faces.

"Are you suggesting we'd touch his stuff?" demanded the doctor.

"Not in the ordinary way, certainly not," I corrected myself. "It just seemed to me — "

"Well, it seemed wrong," he cut in. "You don't know the profession, or you wouldn't even hint at such a possibility.

Another man's kit is sacrosanct. We would no more think of touching each other's personal bag than we would of — of stealing a man's wallet."

"On top of which," added Halloran, "we each keep our own keys, just so some outsider doesn't go poking around."

I was looking at three pairs of stony eyes now, and realised I was trampling on sacred ground.

"You'll have to excuse my ignorance," I pleaded. "Just put it down to non-professionalism. Forget I ever said it."

They shrugged, nodding.

"A natural mistake, Mr. Preston," Tripp assured me. "Now then, what else can we show you?"

I thought rapidly over the supposed basis of my visit, but couldn't think of any area I hadn't covered.

"No, I think not. I've seen enough to satisfy me, from my purely amateur standpoint. Enough for my report anyway. Off the record, I must tell you all that I can't recall having visited any place that was so well-prepared and scrupulously maintained. Thank you all for your co-operation."

The thaw, which Tripp had started, was now completed by the tribute. They all smiled happily as I went out, and found my way back to Filby's office. One of his assistants gave me an anxious frown.

"The Chief was called away, just a few minutes ago," he explained.

"That's too bad," I looked at my watch significantly. "Did he give any indication of how long he might be?"

"No, he didn't seem to know himself."

The assistant was clearly at a loss to know whether he was expected to keep me there or not. I made the decision for him.

"I'll just have to leave a message," I announced, "I have another appointment in town for six-thirty. Will you tell the Chief for me, that I reported, A.O.K., on the situation? He'll know what you mean."

"Will do," he replied.

I left then. I had an appointment alright, but the other party didn't know about it yet. A certain Jack Griswold was about to receive a visitor. The duty roster in the E.M.U., carried home addresses and telephone numbers of all rostered personnel, and I'd memorised the entry opposite Griswold J, before leaving the unit.

The way I looked at it, Griswold J, had some explaining to do.

6

GRISWOLD lived in a small apartment block in a quiet residential section. I found it without much difficulty, and noted the surroundings as I locked up the car. Not fancy, but not rundown either. A good solid type of citizen lived here, would be my assessment, and the rentals would probably be appropriate for someone in Griswold's line of work. Most of the parked cars were a couple of years old, no gleaming Caddies on view, but no wrecks either. Everything seemed about right. The Griswold apartment was on four, and I realised as I went up that I didn't even know whether or not the guy was married. He might even have kids, and the whole family would be sitting down to supper when the strange man pinged the bell.

At the fourth floor, I stepped out

into confusion. I had expected the usual narrow corridor, with anonymous doors either side, the occasional muffled sounds of television sets, family arguments, crying babies. That was what I expected. What I got was something more like Conquest Street on a Saturday night. People were milling around, grouped in open doorways, chattering like magpies. Half a dozen different stations poured out their messages from the apartment interiors, kids were weaving in and out on skates, skate-boards, anything on wheels. Somebody had let the dinner burn, and the sharp smell pervaded the general atmosphere. If I'd been hoping to arrive unnoticed, I was due for a disappointment. Every eye in the place swivelled towards the opening elevator doors, and I found myself as the saying goes, the cynosure of all eyes. Eyes that regarded me with suspicion, hostility, scorn or just plain curiosity, according to the owner's interpretation of my place in the scheme of things. My first impression, that all the doors were ajar, was wrong. There was one which was firmly in position, and in front of it stood a large man, ditto. He wore a faded khaki uniform with a large revolver on his hip, and a star on his chest, reading M.C.P.D., and he stood gradually straighter as I approached. We'd seen each other the moment I'd stepped out of the elevator, which had caused me to cancel my immediate reaction to take to the stairs, and return when all the fuss had died away.

"What do you want here?"

There was ginger hair sprouting on the hand which rested negligently one inch from the open flap of his gun holster.

"Calling on a Mr. Griswold," I replied. "What's going on here?"

He ignored that, tapping with his heel on the closed door, which was opened promptly, and another cop stared out.

"Here's a man calling on Mr. Griswold," announced the man outside.

"Wait right there," instructed the man inside, and went away.

"He says — "

"I heard what he said," I cut in, "and you still didn't tell me what's going on."

"It's my memory," he explained. "I'm thinking of going into therapy. What's your name, buddy?"

"Preston. And yours?"

"Just call me officer."

There was evidently going to be a deficit of any deep philosophical discussion between us, so we just looked at each other till the door opened again, and another man appeared. No uniform this time, just a plain dark suit, topped off by an all-too familiar face.

"Well, well, look who's here," he greeted. "Where are your manners, officer? We don't keep people like Mr. Preston standing out in the hall. Have him come in."

"Hallo Schultzie."

Detective Second Grade Schultz was from Homicide, and that did not bode too well. He stood aside long enough for me to get in, then closed the door.

We were in a tiny hallway, with three doors leading off, but he didn't offer to conduct me any further.

"What's all this about?" I queried.

"Uh, uh," he negatived, waving an admonitory finger. "You trying to cost me my job, or something? I'm Schultz, from headquarters, remember? The tax payers expect me to ask questions, not answer them. Let's put things on their proper footing. Now, you first. What are you doing here?"

"Came to see a man named Griswold," I said reluctantly.

"What about?"

"That's between him and me."

"You think so? Stay here a minute."

He disappeared through one of the open doors, leaving me to inspect the Griswold decor. It didn't run to much, just one large colored picture of the beach at Acapulco, stuck up on the wall, the edges still ragged from its having been torn out of a magazine. That's what I should have done, I realised, when I'd been out at the airport. I should have put myself on a flight to Acapulco while I had the chance. Somebody ought to have told me.

"Preston, as I live and breathe," greeted another familiar voice. "Good of you to drop in."

Detective Sergeant Gil Randall stood blocking the doorway, and beaming at me with false bonhomie. Randall is not just large, he overflows. If I had to guess at his weight I'd make him around two hundred twenty pounds, spread around his six feet two inches. A slow-moving man, never hurried. He has a heavy-jowled sleepy-looking face, with eyes recessed deeply into folds of creased skin. You can tell just by looking at him that his thinking is as slow as his movements, and that the only explanation for him holding down his job has to be that he's first cousin to the mayor. You don't have to take my word for it. Just call in at any of the jails within fifty miles. They're full of people who simply don't understand how they got there, when all they had needed to do was to spin this Randall a tale. He didn't fool me with that hayseed expression. I'd seen him at work too often, seen that impenetrable bulk move with the speed and agility of a ballet dancer when the chips were down. As for his rusty mind, I've known computers that were slower to come up with answers. A very formidable proposition, my old friend Randall, and one of the last people I wanted to run into at that moment.

"Hallo Gil. I seem to have walked into something."

"You do, don't you?" he agreed jovially. "Yes, that would seem to be the situation here. Now, let me recall, last time I heard you were one of those private investigators, big detective, all that stuff. Let's see how good you are. Let us have your opinion about what you might have walked into."

I pretended to think about it.

"Well, this is just off the cuff, you

understand. Running up a flag, in a manner of speaking. What have we here? Uniformed cop on the outside, two people from Homicide in the inside? You appreciate that I'm just guessing wild?"

"Understood." He was enjoying himself, which made one of us.

"I'd say somebody was dead," I finished.

"Bravo," Randall smiled at Schultz. "Told you he was a big detective. Now then, any ideas as to who it might be?"

It would have been a mistake to say Griswold. That would have led direct to another question, which was, why would I think anybody would want to kill Griswold?

"You got me there," I confessed.

Randall looked disappointed.

"Maybe you're not as good as I had you pegged," he grumbled. "You do know whose apartment this is, I fancy? What are you doing here else?"

"Man named of Griswold," I stated,

"but that doesn't mean he has to be dead. Could be anybody."

"H'm. But you did come to see Mr. Griswold, presumably?"

"I did."

"O.K. Come on in and see him."

He vacated the doorway and I went reluctantly through. Two men who must have been lab technicians were busily moving around in what seemed to be the living room, but I hardly noticed them. I was all taken up with another man, who wasn't moving at all. He lay on the floor, where blood had seeped into the carpet from a number of holes in his chest. The blood was too fresh for him to have been there very long. The flowered shirt made me think of Acapulco again. Here was someone else who would have been better advised to buy a ticket.

"Recognise him?" demanded Randall.

"Never saw him before," I denied.

"You sure? Take a very good look. You're sure you don't know him?"

"I already looked, and I still don't know him."

"I see. Then let me introduce you. That is Mr. Griswold, the man you came to visit. And you still don't know him?"

"Right," I confirmed.

"You're just one of these people who goes around visiting with strangers. Kind of pastime, a hobby, you might say?"

"It was nothing important," I hedged, "no big deal."

"The only thing I like about that," snapped Randall, "is your use of the past tense. You said 'was'. It wasn't important, no big deal. But it is now, Preston. I would say it's very important all of a sudden. Man gets himself bumped off, and lo — who is this knock-knocking at the door but a certain P.I., who has come to talk about no big deal. I think you might have something very interesting to tell us. What did you want to talk with him about?"

I looked at the men from the police laboratory, then at the impassive face of the listening Schultz.

"It's kind of private."

"Ah. Secrets, eh? Don't know that I care for that. You see, what we have here is what we call a murder situation. A man is dead. Somebody killed him. We are all getting paid to find out who. Now, look at it from our point of view. How's it going to look on the report, if it says that a man named Preston called in, explained that his business was private, and we didn't like to pry? How is that going to read? I work for a very nice man, very reasonable man, name of Rourke, you may have heard it? Now, how is he going to feel if I put a thing like that on his desk? I don't like to be thought of as an inquisitive person, but I'm going to have to insist."

There was no point in trying to bluff Randall. There never is. What I was facing was twenty-four hours incommunicado, if I didn't co-operate.

195

Randall had the authority to do that, and he wouldn't hesitate.

"Let's take a look out the window," I suggested, walking across.

He hesitated, then followed me, staring out at the concrete towers, windows glinting in the rays of the setting sun. I spoke scarcely above a whisper.

"There could be some connection with the terrorist thing."

A pause, while he took this in, ruminated on it. I had put him in a spot, and I knew it. Every law agency would have a top priority rating on anything connected with what had happened at the airport. Certainly it would take precedence over a routine homicide, which was what this had appeared to be, up until that point. Randall came to a decision. Stepping clear of me he said "Well, I don't know about you, Preston, but I'm finding it stuffy in here. There's a little place across the street. Let's you and me go and have a beer."

Even the lab people stopped and looked at him.

"I thought you weren't supposed to drink on duty?" I parried.

"Absolutely not," agreed the big man. "I would certainly hope not. However, I am now going off duty. I've seen all I need here, and Detective Schultz can wrap it up for me. I'll be back on duty one hour from now, and I'll see you downtown."

He was talking to his partner, who nodded, watching me and wondering. Wondering what it was I'd said that prompted Randall to want to talk with me in private. Well, let him wonder. Five minutes later, the big man was spilling over a narrow stool at the further end of a quiet bar. I parked next to him, and he let me pay for the drinks. There were very few people in the place, and none of them within earshot, but we conducted the entire conversation in low tones that wouldn't have disturbed a mouse.

"You have the floor," he growled.

"First, tell me this," I suggested. "Do you know who Griswold was? I mean, his occupation and so forth?"

"Not yet," he admitted, "we hadn't been there above twenty minutes when you showed. Some kind of medic, by the looks of things. We found medical supplies in the place, stuff like that. No wallet, no keys, not much paper except for a few private letters. Talk about him."

"You're right about the medic aspect," I confirmed. "Jack Griswold is one of the emergency medical unit staff out at Monkton Airport. More than that, he was one of the crew in attendance at the bomb scare yesterday afternoon."

"Zasso?"

He affected only mild interest, but I've seen him work before, and he didn't fool me. He was analysing every word.

"You don't seem very excited," I complained.

Heavy eyes inspected me with amusement.

"Excited?" he queried. "What about? I haven't heard anything yet. Specifically, I haven't heard what makes all this any of your put-in. Try expanding on that."

This was no time for me to be changing stories. I pitched him the same yarn I'd given to Chief Filby a few hours earlier.

"That's a very interesting yarn," he proclaimed, when I finished. "Of course, the airport people will confirm this?"

"Go right to the top," I encouraged. "The Chief of Security himself. Name of Filby."

"I know his name and I'll check. So really, if I'm to believe you, and I didn't say I do, you only have kind of a side interest in this Griswold? I mean, he had no contact with Passenger Howe, the way you tell it."

"That's right," I agreed. "I have no reason to disbelieve what the other members of the team told me, but you know how it is with something

199

this big. All I wanted from Griswold was his corroboration of what they told me happened out there."

"H'm," Randall was quiet for a moment, and I couldn't tell whether he was doubting what I was telling him, or whether that labyrinthine mind of his was diverting the information down new channels. "You are making me think strange thoughts. Let's suppose for a moment I believe you. This is just supposing, you understand. What if something had gone wrong with Passenger Howe, and those two guys you saw today didn't want you getting near Griswold? Maybe he did see something, and they knew it. They wouldn't want him talking to you about it, not after they learned you were sniffing around. What's to prevent one of those people from paying Old Jack a little visit, leave a few holes in him?"

I shrugged.

"Theoretically, nothing. Except they were both on duty when I left, and they don't get through until midnight.

Those people just can't walk in and out when they feel like it. It would take at least an hour to get here and back from the airport. That's a long time to say you were in the john."

"Yes, it is," he agreed sadly. "Try this, then. You say some rival combine is hiring you — "

" — I didn't say that," I objected.

" — you're allowing me to assume it, which amounts to the same thing. What about the other combine, the people who are the present suppliers? They could have foreseen that some busybody — no offense — would get himself hired for just that reason. They could have hired somebody themselves, to go around to this Griswold's place, and plant some adulterated serum in his bag, then claim that the whole shift must have been using stuff which had become contaminated after delivery. That would let them out. What do you think?"

It was an odd situation to be in. Here I was, sitting in a bar, while

Randall tossed out theories off the top of his head. Always assuming he wasn't just playing with me, which is never a safe assumption with that particular officer.

"Pretty far-fetched," I observed. "We're talking about business-men, not mobsters. Even if they came up with a crackpot scheme like that, they would send a man with a handful of money, not a gun."

He was non-commital about that.

"Probably. But somebody was looking for something, and they were certainly interested in the medical side. Like I told you, there was stuff everywhere. Hypodermics, bandages, you name it. Tossed all over the place."

"Is the serum missing?" I asked.

"Dunno," he confessed. "I didn't make up the list of exactly what was found. It'll be on my desk though, by the time I get back to the office. You can bet I'll be looking at it."

"How about drugs?" I suggested brightly. "Maybe a junkie got to him.

Man in that line of work, it's always possible he'll be carrying morphine, cocaine, stuff like that. Worth money on the street."

"Yes it is," he nodded, "and we're looking into that possibility."

"Mind if I ask you a question?" I looked at him sideways. "How come you people got there so fast? He hadn't stopped bleeding all that long before I arrived, and you'd been there twenty minutes then. Told me so yourself."

"No harm in telling you," he shrugged. "A neighbor heard the shots. Lady who lives in the next apartment. She's ex-Army, and she's heard guns before. She knew it wasn't any television program. She called in right away, then watched the corridor to see if anybody came out. Smart lady, that one. Got a good look at a man who left the Griswold place, and came up with a description worth having for once. Right this minute she's going through the mug files. If our man is there, I don't think she'll miss him. A few more citizens like her, and we could cut staff."

The lady next door had evidently made a profound impression on a certain sergeant of detectives.

"She certainly sounds like a good witness."

"Yeah," then almost casually, "why did you say this could tie in with the bomb?"

I've been around long enough not to come up with what some people call guilty starts, but I felt a momentary uneasiness.

"All I meant was, with him being one of the emergency crew and everything, maybe he had seen or heard something that could lead you people to this whatsit, this O.P.A."

"Be your age, Preston. The man would have been grilled last night until he could scarcely stand-up, by everybody from the F.B.I., downwards. Or upwards, depending on your point of view. Don't you think they'd have spotted it?"

"Certainly," I hastened to agree. "If he meant them to know it."

"What's that supposed to mean?" he demanded.

"All I'm thinking is this. Let's say the late lamented saw something out there that could give him a lead on the bombers, only he doesn't want to hand it to the law. He might see a nice little profit in it for himself. Little blackmail, if you follow me."

"I'm ahead of you, and you have a nasty mind," he grumbled. "But I don't buy it on practical grounds. If he tried to pull a stunt like that, yes, they'd probably kill him. It wouldn't bother those guys, when you consider they were quite willing to murder about fifty total strangers. Besides, knocking off a blackmailer isn't even murder, the way some people look at it."

"Well, then?"

"Well, this. Those people wouldn't have cared about the medical stuff. They would just kill him and out. They wouldn't even have taken a chance by going to the apartment in the first place. Most probably, they'd have just blown him away the minute he got out of his car. Why should they run the risk of elevators, stairways, neighbors, all that hassle? No. The man who killed Griswold had a reason to be in that apartment, because he thought there could be something there he wanted."

Like a quarter of a million dollars in missing diamonds, I supplemented. But I didn't want to bother Randall with that. Instead I suggested an alternative.

"Or wanted to substitute," I offered. "You know the theory about leaving some contaminated serum with the third member of the team?"

He shook his head decisively.

"I didn't like it the first time around, and I don't like it any better now."

"But it was your idea," I protested.

"Was it? I don't remember," he denied. "Well, if you're not going to confess to anything I can't spend any more time sitting around in bars. What'll you do now?"

I looked at the wall-clock. It was almost seven thirty. Although I was certain I was wasting my time, I still had that call to make on Dr. Diana Morrison.

"Look at the time. Amazing how it flies when you're enjoying yourself. Tell you the truth, Gil, there is a lady — "

"Might have known it," he snorted. "You don't improve much do you? Bars, dames. It's all a big-roller coaster to you."

"Just so I can meet the tab," I returned frostily.

We got down off our stools. Randall tapped me with a finger the size of a truncheon.

"If I find you've been holding out on me over this, you will live to regret it," he promised. "If you survive to live, that is."

"Listen, you may not have much of an opinion of me, but you know I'm not dumb enough to fool around with anything like this O.P.A. But you won't be the first to know if I come up with anything."

"Really? You trying to hurt my feelings?"

"No. But the vacancy is filled. There's a man name of Witchley, a nasty mean-looking man, who also happens to be an agent of the federal government. He's sort of hoping I'll tell him first, and I sort of intend to, because believe me, I play no games with those people."

"Glad to hear it. Well, I mustn't keep some poor woman from her questionable pleasures. I'll see you."

We emerged into the darkening street, and went to find our respective cars. I waved him goodbye as he climbed in, then set about locating a telephone.

* * *

Dr. Morrison was at home, and no, she had no objection to my calling at eight-fifteen. When I saw the lady, I realised she would have no objection to anyone calling, hour immaterial, so long as the caller was male, and preferably under eighty years old. She received me, as you might put it, informally. Yes, that would cover it, informally. Not that there was much cover on offer. There was a two-inch strip of black material fighting a losing battle to protect the heavy breasts, then quite a lot of the rest of Doctor Morrison before we reached a pair of green ski-pants which had been clearly painted on her, the paint running out well below the navel. I would have been quite content to conduct our conversation on the porch, but she wasn't having any of that. It was almost thirty minutes later when I finally made it, gasping for breath, to the freedom of the night air. By that time, I would gladly have pinned on the amorous lady chemist any crime in the calender for which I could produce a shred of evidence. Unfortunately for my inclinations, she was entirely clean on the scare at the airport. The reason for her late booking had been that she was a last minute substitute for a colleague whose wife had been taken suddenly ill, and he hadn't wanted to leave town. It took me about thirty seconds to establish that crucial fact, and the rest of the time to convince the lady that was the only reason for my call. I could still hear the shrill accusation keening through the night air when I got to the car and stopped running.

"Fagg — ot."

I was so thankful to be out of there, it didn't even offend me. By nine o'clock, I was safely back at Parkside, showered and changed, and wondering what else I could do that night that might be useful. There didn't seem to be very much. Not that was useful. Other alternatives came to mind though, especially the fact that I was now the proud possessor of Candy Sullivan's home number.

She answered on the third ring, recognised my voice and said lightly.

"Oh, hi. You want to change the arrangements for tomorrow?"

"Not really," I confessed. "Right now, I was thinking of changing them this evening."

"Ah," she paused then added. "What kind of change did you have in mind?"

"Well, for one thing, I'm over here and you're over there," I pointed out. "I thought we might change that. Have you eaten yet?"

"I had some milk toast a couple of hours ago. I have to watch my figure."

"Listen, I know a place where they have steaks you can cut with a fork. Why don't we go there, and while you're eating, I'll keep an eye on your figure for you?"

She chuckled, and I liked it.

"I don't know," she demurred, "I wouldn't want to be late getting home. There's this terrible man I work for, and I have to keep on my toes. Where is this eating-house?"

"It's called El Burro, down on

Twenty-Third," I said hopefully.

"An original idea," she replied, "I don't believe I ever had a donkey steak before. Is it legal?"

"That's just the name. The meat is all prime beef. Are we going?"

"I wouldn't want to be misunderstood," and her tone was serious. "If I come out to eat steak, that's all I'm coming for. Agreed?"

"You got it," I promised. "Besides, I have this dragon of a secretary. I couldn't face her in the morning if I'd mis-behaved. She'd know at once. Do I come and get you?"

"No thanks. I'll take a cab. Nine-thirty?"

"I'll be waiting."

I was, too. I got there in record time and had a little chat with Sancho, who doubles as proprietor and head waiter. A highly romantic character, is Sancho, and when I explained what a very special lady I was bringing to his joint, he bent over backwards to make arrangements.

When Candy Sullivan walked in, the place went into a freeze-frame for a few seconds. Me too, until it penetrated that this gorgeous object was actually coming to meet me. Then I sprang forward, hands outheld. She took them in hers, and smiled.

"Hi, Mark."

"Mark? We progress."

"It's after five," she reminded me.

She wore a halter-neck scoop fronted dress of white cotton, a simple little creation that yelled money. The gleaming black hair was brushed back behind her ears, which sported the deepest green emeralds, her only jewellery. The rich bronze of her arms and shoulders was emphasised by the whiteness of the dress.

"I might need them for eating?" she suggested.

I was still holding onto her hands, I realised, and let them go with a reluctant sigh.

"They managed to find us a quiet table," I announced leading her inside.

All the men pretended not to be looking at her, and all the women pretended not to notice the men pretending. Well, let them look, I decided magnanimously. It wasn't every day the common people got a real close-up of a goddess. Sancho was lurking around waving menus and napkins.

"This is my friend Sancho," I introduced, "he owns the place."

"A pleasure, senor."

She held out a hand man-fashion, but he grabbed it and bent his lips to it, Spanish-fashion.

"An honour, senorita."

What with that, and her black hair, and the brilliant smile she let fly at him, Sancho was her slave from then on. He clicked his fingers, and clapped his hands, and a small army of waiters zoomed in and out.

Candy ordered her steak and salad, and I settled for the same. I picked up the wine-list, but Sancho begged me to let him take care of it.

214

"There is a little wine, Mr. Preston, which does not appear on the list. It is kept in my special stock for special occasions."

I shrugged, and let him get on with it. We lit cigarets, and she peeked at the brand.

"I might have known you'd smoke Old Favorites," she confided, in that husky voice of hers. "You like to have the best of everything don't you?"

"You have to admit I do well at it," I returned. "After all, you're here."

She treated me to one of those lazy smiles.

"I like your friend Sancho. Do you come here a lot?"

What she meant was, did I bring a lot of females to the place. I shook my head.

"Not too much," I denied. "Lincoln's birthday, gala occasions. You know."

"This isn't Lincoln's birthday," she pointed out, "so what's the gala occasion?"

"Miss Sullivan," I announced, very

215

formal, "in that dress, you are one walking gala occasion."

Her eyes held mine for a moment, then she looked down.

"Tell me what you've been up to all day."

"First you tell me something," I evaded. "Do you have any medical qualifications?"

"That's an odd one," she frowned. "The answer is no, but why do you ask?"

"Because I'm up to here in doctors," I confessed. "I seem to have run into no other kind of person all day long, and I was beginning to think there weren't any ordinary people around. Not even a first aid badge in the girl scouts?"

"Not even that," she assured me, "I failed a chemistry exam once. Not exactly Madame Curie in embryo. Why so many doctors?"

I told her a few little bits and pieces, leaving out names and reasons. Just enough to satisfy her curiosity, without her being able to fit any kind of pattern to it all.

"Last call was on this female chemist, at least that's what she calls herself. Personally, I suspect she's an anatomist in disguise."

I told her about my trip out to Settler's Avenue, where the man-eating Dr. Morrison had her lair, and how I had to fight my way out of the place. She seemed to enjoy the story, and laughed a few times.

"I don't believe a word of it," she refuted, when I'd finished. "The poor woman probably had to lock herself in the bathroom to get away from you."

"She called me a — " I looked around, lowering my voice " — a faggot. That's what she called me."

That seemed to delight her.

"She really said that?"

"Said it?" I echoed. "She hollered it out at the top of her lungs. I could still hear her two blocks away."

"So you went home and called me," she pointed out, and with unwanted accuracy. "Is that what I'm doing here, restoring your injured masculine pride?"

I realised I had been led neatly into one of those deadly verbal traps some women are so good at, and hastened to repair the damage.

"You are here because I wanted to be with you, outside of the office. That was what I wanted from the moment I first laid eyes on you. Did you know you saved me from a lifetime of speculation?"

"No, and I don't know what that means. Could you expand on it?"

I told her about my first glimpse of her, jammed as I had been at the rear of the elevator that morning, when all I could see of her was the upper half. She didn't quite purr, but she evidently liked it.

"But I'm only here to eat," she reminded me. "Those were the terms."

"Still are," I promised. "And speaking of that, here comes the food."

My beautiful companion might be

watching her figure, as she claimed, but she hadn't forgotten how to dispose of the edibles. There was none of your fancy picking. The Sullivans were evidently a well-established line of steak-eaters, and the present generation, in the person of Candy, was a credit to her forebears. Sancho had excelled himself, and he'd been quite right about the wine. It was from his private stock, no question about it. We didn't talk much, but it wasn't necessary. I think she was as conscious as I was of a gradual building of atmosphere between us, and it had a momentum of it's own. Too much chatter would have been superfluous, an intrusion.

By the time we reached the coffee, we were thoroughly relaxed. She wouldn't take any brandy, and neither did I. It was Candy who put it into words.

"After food and wine of this quality," she explained, "anything else would be too much. Perfect is perfect, and it should be left alone."

There was no arguing with that and

I nodded seriously.

"Agreed. And this has been as perfect an evening as I can recall."

Her eyes had a way of lighting up at the corners when she smiled.

"I'll bet you say that to all the gala occasions. But it has been lovely, and I really want to thank you. And now, I must go."

"Go?"

"It's eleven thirty," she explained, "and I have to get the glass slippers back before midnight."

"If you say so," I agreed regretfully. "I'll get the check."

"No." She put a restraining hand on my arm. "I don't want you to take me home. Not this time. Just ask Sancho to arrange a cab for me."

There is a time to argue and a time to let things happen. Some people go through their whole lives without ever learning this simple rule. I was one, for a long time, until experience taught me better. I waved to Sancho, and he went off to make the call.

"You win," and I even smiled, like a good loser. "Mark you, I don't know where we're going to find any frogs to pull milady's carriage. Not at this hour of the night."

"Horsepower will be fine," she assured me, leaning over and patting me softly on the hand. "Thank you for tonight. You'll ask me again, won't you?"

"Would tomorrow be too soon?" I countered.

"Don't rush me, Mark," she counselled gravely. "I'll see you at the office in the morning. And thank you again."

Soft lips brushed lightly at my cheek, and she was gone in a faint trail of perfume. Sancho came back to the table, and eyed me with concern.

"Everything is well, with you and the lady?" he asked gently.

I got up to leave, considering the question.

"I wish I knew, Sancho. I wish I knew."

7

THE next morning I rolled out of bed with reluctance, then remembered that I'd be seeing Candy at nine o'clock. Strictly on duty, of course, but it was sufficient to dispel my natural lethargy. While the coffee-pot was grouching away, I put on the answering machine to find out what had come through the previous evening, feeling guilty about it. Guilty, because I knew perfectly well I ought to have had a listen before I went to bed, but I had chosen not to do that. My mind was still full of Candy Sullivan, and I didn't want a lot of intrusive outsiders butting into my reverie. They would still be there next morning, I reasoned, and I was right.

They certainly were.

There were five calls in all, but from two people only. One was my client, J. J. Fontaine. He didn't use his name, but there was no mistaking the voice. All he said was, he hoped things were progressing satisfactorily, and that I should call his office the next morning to make an interim report. Mr. Fontaine had been too long in the world of legitimate business, I decided. Just how do people make interim reports about things like bomb-maniacs, jewel thefts and now murder? What is an interim report anyway? Presumably it means that somebody tells somebody else that he still hasn't finished what he's supposed to do, but he's working on it. Well, I could certainly claim that, and made a mental note to call the man from the office.

The other four calls were all from Agent Witchley, on a rising tide of impatience at being unable to get any response. In the end he was reduced to muttering darkly about having me brought in if he didn't get some answers. He also said that if I couldn't get him at the number

I'd tried previously, I was to call the main office. They would know how to contact him, and presumably somebody in my line of work would be able to find the number without his help.

I knew the number all right, and I didn't wait until office time before calling it. The main office of the Federal Bureau of Investigation is tucked away on the top four storeys of the seventeen-storey Federal building at 11000 Wiltshire Boulevard, and those people never sleep. Despite the early hour, I punched out 272 6161, and waited. Not long.

"F.B.I.," came a crisp female voice, "who's calling please?"

"Name is Preston, Mark Preston," I told her. "Agent Witchley is trying to get in touch with me, and vice versa. He's a member of the Major Case Squad, and he's dealing with this terrorist attempted bomb attack at Monkton City Airport."

"I'll put you through to that extension," she decided.

This time I got a man, and I went through the rigmarole again. He listened courteously, then said, "Is your business urgent, would you say?"

I thought about that before replying.

"No, I don't think it's urgent," I admitted. "It's important, but not urgent. What's the point?"

"Just this, Mr. Preston. Agent Witchley clocked off at four a.m., today, and he's a little short on sleep. If your call was urgent, I wouldn't let a little thing like his necessary rest put you off. But if it could wait, a couple of hours, I think he'd probably appreciate it."

Considering that Witchley was probably already out of sorts with me, I didn't want to be the cause of dragging him out of bed. It wouldn't be calculated to make him love me any more.

"Let the man sleep," I suggested. "I'll probably be in my own office later this morning. We'll catch each other then."

"Got it. Thank you for your call."

I held the phone for a few seconds, wondering what it was that had kept Witchley busy until the small hours. The clattering of the percolator told me that there was coffee ready and waiting, and I went thankfully to it. The time was eight twenty and, allowing a fifteen minute drive to the office, in order to open up at nine o'clock, I had a whole twenty-five minutes to myself. It could be my only opportunity that day for any restful contemplation. Once I got outside, into that big world out there, I would be chivvied hither and thither by chance, force of circumstance, and of course, people. Somebody once said the world would be a wonderful place to live in, if it weren't for all the people. At times, I have to concede he had a point.

Coffee within reach, I sat down to clarify the vague thoughts which had been chasing each other around in my head for the past twenty-four hours.

The key-figure, so far, had to be the substitute para-medic, Jack Griswold, now deceased. I wished I had had just five minutes alone with the man, before the killer beat me to it. Griswold had made it on to that particular shift by default, or so the story went. I didn't buy that, anymore than I believed Lawrence's stomach upset was a coincidence. It had been intended that Lawrence should be unfit for duty, and that Griswold should take his place. The point was, why? Flight 147 was scheduled for a four o'clock departure, the precise hour at which the emergency teams changed shifts. As it chanced, smog unpredictable smog, had kept the aircraft on the ground over that crucial time-period. The bomb-warning, delivered when the plane was supposed to be miles in the sky, in fact came in time for the bomb to be de-activated and all the passengers and crew disembarked in safety. So why Griswold? There has never yet been a terrorist or thief born who could forecast the arrival of smog.

I was confident by this time that

Griswold had been responsible for the theft of the diamonds. Griswold had been the substitute, Griswold had been the one to see the necessity for drugging Walter M. Keane, and Griswold had now been eradicated by someone who had searched the apartment for something of value. He was my man, dead or not, but how and why? Then, I began to get a glimmering of an idea. Suppose Griswold was the standby thief, the silent partner, only to be used in case of emergency? I tried to put myself into the mind of whoever planned the operation, bearing in mind that we were talking about a quarter of a million dollars. A caper that size is worthy of some serious forethought. I thought I might plant my main thief on the passenger list. His — or her — job would be to effect the theft any time from touchdown in Boston onwards. But in case something should go wrong, I had a second man in reserve on the ground. Griswold. What could possibly go wrong? Well, for one thing, the captain could get taken suddenly sick, the aircraft itself could be adjudged unfit to fly at the last moment. A delay would follow. Airlines don't keep rows of bench-substitute captains sitting around waiting for cancellations. Replacement at that level takes time. Similarly with an unserviceable airplane. People just don't hop out of one and on to another. Again, it takes time. Then there was the thief himself. He could miss the flight, get held up in traffic, drop dead of a heart attack. The more I thought about it, the more I liked the idea of a second man, on the ground, ready to step in if the first man, for whatever reason, looked like failing. That too, would account for the need to have Griswold cover both shifts. It was an emergency move, only intended to bear fruit if the emergency arose.

Crossing to the percolator for more coffee, I found myself getting happier by the minute. No one could have foreseen the combination of the attempted explosion plus smog. But any intelligent planner would allow for some kind, any kind, of unforeseen delay. And that man would plan for it. He couldn't plant a substitute on both shifts, but he could arrange for someone to slip the unfortunate Lawrence a Michael Finn, and there was the vacancy, with Griswold waiting to fill it. I began to elaborate on it. If I had been arranging all this, would I necessarily have told Griswold the identity of the main operative? Probably not, I decided. In the thief business it doesn't always pay to let the left hand know what the right hand is doing. No. Griswold's brief would be simple. If anything went wrong on Flight 147, it was his job somehow to get to Passenger Keane, and relieve him of the jewel-case.

Then why did they kill him? The only answer seemed to be the oldest in the world. Griswold, finding himself in sudden possession of all those stones, had decided on a double-cross. Or even a higher fee. One way or another, he had tried a hold-out, and now he was dead. Although I was becoming more and more enamoured of my reasoning, I didn't like the conclusion which followed inevitably. It meant that my next job would have to be to find the killer, and then who hired him, and that was not a task I contemplated with any relish at all. Up until now, I'd got away with sticking my nose in, here there and everywhere, on the basis of a trumped-up yarn, in which the hole card was Daniel P. Howe and his suffering. It wasn't easy to see how I could suddenly extend my terms of reference to take in the murder of Jack Griswold. The connection was at it's very best, tenuous. At it's worst, it was non-existent. It was a thoughtful journey into the city.

I beat Candy to the office by better than two minutes, and was seated at my own desk, when I heard her arrive. After dumping stuff on her desk, she came and stuck her head around the door.

"Morning Mr. Preston," she greeted, straight-faced.

"Morning, Candy," two could play at that game, "I already have the post. There's nothing worth reading so far."

"Okay," she replied cheerfully. "I'll get on with the newspapers."

Shamefaced, I remembered I hadn't checked up on the situation chez Digby. I made the call, learned that things were coming along nicely, and that she hoped to be back at her desk on Monday. I tried to respond to that cheerfully, but the prospect of Candy-less Monday was not one I wanted to dwell on. Then I put through another call, this time to J. J. Fontaine, to make the requisite interim report. The lady I knew only as Myrtle answered, and put me through to him right away. There was a light click, as he picked up the telephone, then the smallest suggestion of a background hiss before he spoke.

"Good morning. How are things going?"

"Will you just hold a minute, Mr. Fontaine?" I put the receiver down gently on the desk and tip-toed over to the door, peeking round. Candy was busy chopping up news items, and her telephone was well out of reach. It seemed to be my day for feeling ashamed. I went back, and said to him, "I'm sorry about this, but someone just walked into my office. Call you back in five minutes."

Without giving him time to protest, I hung up. Then I went out to my favorite news-clipper.

"Have to go out," I told her. "With any luck I'll be back between ten-thirty and eleven."

"Very well. Is there somewhere I can reach you?"

Her tone was friendly, but business-like.

"No, I'm just roaming around," I evaded. "See you later."

Down in the lobby I called Fontaine's

number from a public booth. This time I didn't ask for him, but dealt direct with Myrtle.

"Oh this is Preston again. Don't bother putting me through. Will you tell Mr. Fontaine that I'm coming over right away, please? I won't keep him long."

Twenty minutes later I turned into that immaculate driveway, parked, and found Myrtle waiting by the open door. Her face was anxious.

"Good morning Mr. Preston. I do hope this is necessary. Mr. Fontaine has a very tight schedule this morning."

Evidently the boss had burned her ears about my trip out.

"No," I re-assured her, "not long at all. But he'll be pleased that I came, so don't you worry about it."

Nodding hopefully she led the way through to that beautiful room again, where my current employer was standing, watching my arrival.

"I hope this is important, Mr. Preston," he greeted, none too warmly.

"I think so," I waited until my escort was clear of the door, then closed it firmly. "When I called you the first time this morning, I realised we weren't alone. One of us is being bugged, and with so much equipment on the market these days, it's hard to know which. Sorry if my visit isn't convenient, but it's better we speak in person."

"Yes, yes," he agreed faintly, sitting down. "Bugged, you say? But who would have the temerity, the brass impudence — "

"Almost anybody," I assured him. "Especially in my case. Don't forget we're dealing with a terrorist organisation, and the boys on our side want them caught. They're not too scrupulous about procedures in a case like this, and, as a citizen, I really don't blame them. There's no such thing as playing fair when you're after people like that."

"No, no, I agree with that. And, after all, everyone knows you have an involvement, so I suppose one ought not to be too shocked, but," he qualified, "you said this device could be at my end. Why on earth should anyone think I'm involved?"

I heaved my shoulders.

"Who knows? Maybe I was tailed out here on my first visit, and they just don't want to miss out on any possibility. Before I go, I'll leave you the name of a man who will come out here and disinfect the place. He's an electronic genius, and if you have a bug, he'll find it. Might cost you a couple of hundred, but I fancy that won't worry you?"

"No. Naturally not. You'll be using this man yourself, I imagine?"

The smooth face took on a look of surprise when I shook my head.

"No. That would make me a suspicious character. Why should I suddenly want to hide anything, particularly at this moment in time? Being bugged has it's advantages, once you know about it. Not only can you play innocent all the time, but you can turn the coin over. You can plant false ideas in their heads about what you're doing. It keeps them happy, and it avoids them doubling up on surveillance."

Understanding now, he looked happier for a moment. Then, "But if that's true of you, surely it's equally true in my case?"

It was, and there was no point in my denying it.

"That's so," I admitted. "But the plain fact is, in your case it doesn't matter, does it? You're not playing any active part in this. That's why you hired me, to do the rushing around. If they want to waste manpower checking up on you, let them. You've nothing to hide, just business secrets, and I don't think our listening friends will be very interested in them."

The frown, which threatened for a moment to crease his forehead, was quickly gone.

"You are absolutely right, and I have no cause for outrage. As you just pointed out, I too am a citizen.

If catching these madmen means that a few innocent people have their telephones tapped, well, that's just too bad. One ought not to allow one's personal outrage to come into the picture. Very well, I will call this expert of yours. And now, Mr. Preston, what have you got to tell me? Oh, please sit down."

I plonked down opposite, in the same chair I'd occupied before.

"I think I know who stole your property, and how he did it," I announced, for openers.

Fontaine's eyes gleamed briefly, and the ghost of a smile appeared.

"So quickly? The details, if you please."

"Did you ever hear the name Griswold?" I asked. "Jack Griswold? In any connection whatever?"

Silence, while he ran the name through his memory. Although I half-expected it, I was still conscious of disappointment when it came up negative.

"No," he denied, "I don't believe I have. Is he our man?"

"Well, he was, if my theory holds. Somebody killed him yesterday afternoon, before I could get to him."

"Killed?" he repeated. "You mean murdered?"

"Right. Let me tell you what I've been doing."

I gave him an account of my activities the previous day, keeping it down to essentials. Fontaine was a good listener, and didn't once interrupt. When I was through he said, "You really seem to have been most successful. My congratulations."

"It was luck, mostly," I confessed. "People are not usually quite so willing to answer questions, but the various official bodies involved have kind of got them into the habit of it. I was just one more man with some kind of badge."

"You mustn't be over-modest," he admonished. "To have tracked down this man Griswold betokens a wealth of experience and knowledge. So you think whoever killed him now has our property?"

I was still stuck on that 'betokens'. Then I realised he was waiting.

"Er, yes. It seems likely. And I wanted you to know it, because we now have a different situation with the police."

"Different? In what way?"

Sometimes, even with someone as bright as J. J. Fontaine, things have to be spelled out.

"We now have Homicide involved," I explained. "They never heard of our man before yesterday, but that's changed. He is now a cadaver, and that makes him very special. They want to know who killed him, and why. They know the place was turned over, searched that is. The killer was looking for something, but what? I have done my best to persuade them it was drugs, and they'll certainly consider that. But it won't be enough to stop them considering everything else. If

240

that man got his hands on those stones, the police will know it, once they catch up with him. That will be very bad for us all. You, your partners, and more especially, me."

"More especially you?" he queried. "We stand to lose a quarter of a million here. Plus the embarrassment, if everything becomes public knowledge."

I stared at him stony-faced.

"Embarrassment you can survive. The quarter million will hurt, but it won't be the end of you. I stand to lose much more." I paused there, for effect. "I stand to lose my license, Mr. Fontaine, and without that, I'm dead."

"Ah."

Understanding now, he wagged his head slowly up and down in assent. Somewhere outside the open windows, a bird chirped with sudden joy. He'd probably just located some unfortunate worm, and was in process of dragging him out into eating distance, I could visualise the scene. The bird had an uncommon look of Gil Randall about him. It was Fontaine who broke the silence, and, thankfully, the image.

"Your point is well taken," he said softly. "So, it would seem your task in to catch up with whoever shuffled Mr. Griswold off this mortal coil, and to get to him before the police?"

"That's how it stacks."

He pursed his lips, indicating reservations.

"Just now, when you were recounting your exploits, you said the lady who lived next door to him would be able to identify the man."

"I think so, yes. The officer involved, a Sergeant Randall, spoke very well of her. I know Randall, and he's very sparing with his praise. Yes, I would think there's a good chance, if the man is a professional. Every officer on the force will be looking for him."

"If? You said 'if'. And supposing he is not?"

"Well then, she could still identify him, but they have to find him first, and that isn't nearly so easy. We have a distinct edge, if this guy is just another man with a gun."

"Oh? Just explain that to me, if you would," he invited.

"Because we know why," I told him. "It was because of the diamonds. We don't know who was double-crossing who, but we do know why. And it brings us right back to basics Mr. Fontaine."

"Basics?"

"The diamonds are at the bottom of it. Before you can steal something, you have to know it exists. We're back to your own people again. People who knew Walter M. Keane, people who knew he sometimes acted as a courier. That's probably a whole lot of people, but we can reduce the list to a handful. The handful who knew Keane would be using Flight 147. I haven't pushed you on that angle before, because I knew you'd be doing some thinking of your own, without any help from me. My job was to trace the thief and recover the stones. I think I've done the first part, but it isn't enough, because the man is dead. The chances are that your valuables are now with whoever fed Griswold the information in the first place, and I'm in your hands in that area."

He nodded his acquiescence, but he wasn't happy.

"I appreciate that. But my — um — colleagues in this matter are all men of irreproachable stature. Wealthy men, all of them. I'm not saying that any of them would refuse the opportunity of an extra quarter of a million, but then, who would? But to obtain it by those means, and to complicate everything with murder, no, Mr. Preston, I really have thought about this very deeply, and my partners can be ruled out." Then, seeing the expression on my face, he continued. "Don't misunderstand me. I was not born yesterday. I am not taking the view that this could not possibly have been done by someone I know and trust. That would be naive, and I disclaim that. On the contrary, while you have been busy in your way, I have been busy in mine. I have conducted a very thorough investigation of my own, into the up-to-date financial position of everyone connected with this transaction. Believe me, there cannot be the slightest suspicion attaching to any one of them. I'll have to ask you to accept that. It is quite obvious, on today's report, that you do what you do very well. I too have a certain competence, in my own areas, and I have been very thorough, believe me."

I believed him. I didn't want to. I would have preferred him to say that he'd been astonished to learn that old so-and-so was under some financial pressure, and who would have thought it? But he hadn't said that. He'd said he'd checked, and he was satisfied. That meant I was going to have to be satisfied too, however grudgingly.

"I won't pretend I'm not disappointed," I admitted, "but that sounds conclusive. What about your junior partners, office clerks, people who work for your colleagues."

Again he shook his head.

"Not involved," he dismissed. "These affairs are conducted only at the very highest level, and there are no records, no files. The only people who would know about Keane's movements were the people at the meeting. This is not exactly the kind of information we put on notice-boards, Mr. Preston. We are all of us continually conscious of the risks."

"Then that leaves only one possibility within your organisation," I mused.

"What? What's that you're saying?"

"I was thinking out loud," I replied. "Only one person outside your group could have had reason to know where Mr. Keane was bound. Probably some seventeen year old, in her first job. The lowest rung of the ladder, Mr. Fontaine, and I'm kicking myself that I didn't think of it before. Tell me, when one of your people makes a trip, who does the actual work, buys tickets, orders cabs, that kind of thing?"

I was making more sense now, and he was interested.

"In Keane's case, I really wouldn't know," he admitted. "He runs a small office of his own, a handful of staff."

"How about a Girl Friday, like your Myrtle?" I pressed, sensing that I might be onto something.

"There is such a person, I have occasionally spoken to her on the telephone. Name now, let me see." While he was thinking he must have pushed that buzzer again, because Myrtle appeared suddenly behind me.

"Trying to remember the name of Mr. Keane's secretary. Can you help?"

She thought quickly.

"Yes, of course. It's Betty Talmage. You want me to call her?"

"No, oh excuse me."

For a moment there, I'd forgotten this wasn't my office, and it was not for me to give orders. Fontaine nodded.

"Mr. Preston is quite right. The lady is not to be contacted under any circumstances."

Then I had another thought. Top level people like Fontaine and his cronies do not work any five-day week with set hours. They work all hours, if need be, and might want to contact each other at weekends or holidays. For this they would rely on their secretaries on occasions, and it was quite usual for the secretaries to run a kind of back-up service of their own.

"Do you mind if I ask a question, Mr. Fontaine?"

"Please do."

I turned to Myrtle who was clearly fascinated to know what was going on.

"If Mr. Fontaine suddenly wanted to contact Mr. Keane out of hours, and wasn't quite certain where he was, would you be able to help?"

"Usually, yes. I certainly hope so."

Better and better.

"And how would you tackle the problem?" I asked, all conciliatory.

"I should get hold of Mrs. Keane in

the first instance, and if she couldn't help, I would try Betty Talmage."

That was the pay-line, the three symmetrical oranges.

"So you have her home address and telephone number," I smiled silkily.

"Why yes," and my smile seemed to alarm her. "There's nothing wrong is there, Mr. Fontaine? I mean, the only way we can keep our employers in constant touch is for us to be in touch with each other. But for a similar arrangement with his secretary, I would never have been able to contact Mr. Wasserman last month, when you wanted him so urgently."

But the gentle reassurance on Fontaine's face was having it's intended effect of soothing Myrtle's feathers and her voice had returned to it's normal pitch by the time she reached the end of the sentence.

"Perfectly in order, Myrtle, and indeed, I don't really see how else you could operate. Would you be good enough now to let Mr. Preston have a note of the lady's home address and telephone? This whole conversation, by the way, is top priority confidential, you understand?"

"Certainly," she agreed, clearly mollified. "I'll go and do it at once."

After the door was shut, Fontaine looked at me.

"What will you do now?"

"Damned if I know," I admitted. "Just clutching at straws really, but when there's no log in view, you settle for straws. I'll have a word with the Talmage woman, ask a few questions about her. I'm not very hopeful, but at least I'll be doing something. Could I made a suggestion?"

"Of course."

"Women don't mean any harm as a rule, but they do love to talk. I'm sure your Myrtle is entirely trustworthy — "

" — well, I should hope so — "

" — but, just the same, I'd forbid her to use the telephone, for anything at all. You have a first class cover story, Mr. Fontaine. The place is probably bugged, and you'll be sending for this expert. Pending his arrival, no calls. It makes sense, she'll understand that."

"You are an extremely cautious man, Mr. Preston," he observed drily.

"In my business, if you want to stay alive and out of jail, caution is rule number one," I told him, and I meant it. "I'll call you later, from a pay-phone, and find out whether it's safe to talk with you. Or better still, where do you go for lunch? I could call you there. That will be guaranteed safe."

He gave me the number of a private club where I'd probably catch him sometime between one and two o'clock, and I went back out to collect my goodies from Myrtle. She handed over a neatly-typed piece of paper, and I glanced at it quickly.

"I do hope this doesn't mean Betty's in some kind of trouble," she asked diffidently. "She always seems such a very nice competent person. And a great deal to put up with in her private life."

Suddenly, I found I wasn't in a hurry at all.

"Oh, dear," I commiserated, "I'm sorry to hear that. What kind of troubles does she have. Is she a sick lady?"

"God forbid," she replied quickly. "Far from it. There's nothing wrong with Betty Talmage, and she can't afford to have anything go wrong. First of all, there was that ghastly husband of hers. He let her down badly, and left her almost destitute when he finally took off for South America. And good riddance. Then she has this old father, practically bedridden and he takes up all her spare time. Mr. Keane is very good. Whenever he's away, he lets Betty stay home with her father. In his absence there's nothing much for her to do in the office anyway."

It sounded like a familiar tale, and not very promising material for my kind of enquiries.

"And I suppose there's no one else in the family to give her a hand?"

"Might as well not be," she sniffed,

"she has this so-called brother, but he's worthless. The only time she ever sees him is when he wants to borrow money, or to stay over for a few days, because he's been thrown out of some cheap hotel."

I don't know who I felt most sorry for at that moment, the unfortunate Betty Talmage or myself.

"She certainly doesn't have much of a life for a young woman," I offered in sympathy. "Mind you I'm taking a lot for granted, assuming that she's young, I mean."

Myrtle eyed me unsurely.

"She's in her early thirties, I would guess. Might as well be sixty, with the life she leads."

"Well, thank you for this," I slipped the note into my pocket. "I'll be as little trouble to her as I can."

I'd been hoping for a quiet snoop around the Talmage establishment while she was out at work, but Myrtle's information had put paid to that little notion. The place was probably full of relatives, bed-ridden and workshy, plus in the absence of Mr. Keane, Betty herself. Well at least I'd be going in through the front door instead of some casement window. I wouldn't need to burglarise the place.

On the ride into town, I found myself wondering what kind of a woman she was. The way Myrtle told it she would slot in about midway between martyr and saint, and that is no slot for a healthy woman in her early thirties. Suppose she just happened to bump into some man? A plausible, attractive man, who could come up with a little scheme which would put them all on easy street. Proper care for the old man, a new life for Betty, a few bucks to get rid of the brother. All she'd need to do would be to tell this Adonis the date and flight number of Mr. Keane's next trip, and lover-boy would take care of the rest. I liked it when I first thought of it, and I liked it better and better as the miles went by. That was my man, it had to be. A woman in Betty Talmage's position of trust at work, and misery at home, was a perfect set-up for a con-artist.

I actually started to whistle, always a good sign, if not very good for the listeners. As usual, I started on Body and Soul, and as usual I got lost in the middle eight bars, so I switched to something else, and for a moment, I couldn't remember the title. Then it came back to me.

Candy. I was whistling Candy.

Wherever he was, Freud would be chuckling.

8

I'D finished her theme-song by the time I got back to the original article. She pointed to her watch.

"Ten past eleven," she announced. "You're late."

"I was hoping you'd miss me," I said wistfully.

"Oh I did," she replied half-mockingly, "so did your friend Witchley. Have you done something to annoy that man?"

"I hope not." I replied fervently. "Why, what did he say?"

"He said if you didn't manage to contact each other soon, he might have to meet you on Wilshire? What did he mean by that?"

I hesitated fractionally, then decided to tell her.

"He means the Federal Building," I explained. "My friend and close buddy Mr. Witchley, is an F.B.I. Agent.

256

Real name Witchhunt. He thinks I'm avoiding him."

Her eyes widened, then she smiled.

"Oh, I see. Imagine, a real F.B.I., man. And are you? Avoiding him?"

"Hell, no," I denied. "Every time I call either he's not there, or he's in bed. I don't go in for games with these people. They play too rough. Did he say which number would find him?"

"I have it here," she confirmed.

"Get him for me, please."

I poured myself some coffee while she was getting through, making motions to ask whether she wanted some. She shook her head, and I carried the container into my own room, then sat down to wait. The telephone pinged.

"Preston. Is that Mr. Witchley?"

"I would hope so," he growled. "I was beginning to wonder whether either of us really existed. What's going on with you?"

"Not much," I hedged. "I'm just asking questions here and there, hoping something will turn up."

257

"And did it?"

His tone was probing and suspicious.

"No," I denied, sounding resigned. "How about you? You got a line on those people yet?"

"Ve ask ze questions," he returned, all mock-Nazi. Jokes, already. "How's the lady coming along, your secretary's mother?"

You never, know with these people, when a question is as innocent as it sounds. Well, the answer was innocent enough.

"Coming along fine. Miss Digby should be back with me on Monday."

"Oh, so that wasn't her I spoke with just now?"

"No, that's a girl from the agency."

"Really? Nice voice."

"Nice everything," I assured him with feeling.

"Lucky you. Some of us have to work. And talking about that, I hear strange things about you. Like to discuss them. Probably just rumours."

We were getting to the bottom line.

"Oh? What kind of things?"

"Nothing specific," he evaded, "and I wouldn't want to talk on the phone, you never can tell who's listening, these days."

I thought that was cool, coming from him. It had probably been him who had arranged the tap on my number in the first place.

"You want to meet?" I queried. "I have to go out, right now. Could we make it this afternoon some time?"

"I suppose so," and he sounded resigned. "I'll come to you. Shall we say your office at three o'clock?"

"O.K. Should I call a lawyer?"

"Depends on what you've been up to," he side-stepped. "Will I get a look at this nice secretary?"

"Yes, but lay off," I warned, "I saw her first."

There wasn't time to sit around speculating about what he wanted. I unlocked the drawer where I kept the office Colt, and checked the mechanism. There was a quick tap at the door, and Candy Sullivan came in, the smile on her face evaporating when she saw the gun.

"That's a nasty looking thing," she shuddered. "Are you intending to shoot somebody?"

"I hope not," I assured her. "Sometimes it pays to have this thing along, just to discourage people from shooting me."

She nodded, but she still didn't like it.

"You're going out then."

"Right. If I'm not back before, I'll certainly be here at three o'clock. Mr. Witchley is coming to see me, or so he says."

"I don't follow you."

"I suspect he's really coming to look at the owner of a certain beautiful voice. Particularly since I told him the rest of you is a perfect match."

Her face said she was uncertain whether to be flattered or annoyed.

"I'm about through with the newspapers," she told me, changing the subject. "What can I be doing while you're out?"

"There isn't much, I'm afraid. Just hold down the fort and try to keep awake, if you can."

"No chance of coming with you?" she asked, not too hopefully. "I'd like to be in on some real investigating."

"Uh uh," I negatived, holding up the automatic. "You don't seriously for one moment imagine I'm going to take you with me anyplace that I'm also taking this thing? I know it's boring out there, but at least I'll know you're safe."

Her eyes softened at that.

"Does it matter, Mr. Preston?"

"It matters, Miss Sullivan," I assured her, rising from the chair. "And now, I must go."

As I passed her, she put a hand on my arm.

"Be careful."

I patted her hand and paused, but this wasn't the time.

"Don't talk to any strange Witchleys." I admonished, and went.

★ ★ ★

Betty Talmage kept her sick father in a neat little house in a neat little suburb on the desert side of town. There weren't many other cars on view as I drove down the street. This was a neighborhood where people went to work, and the cars went with them. The Talmage car was outside, a four-year old Chev, well cared for. I knew it would be, just like the well-clipped shrubs either side of the pathway as I walked up to the front door. Putting on my most reassuring, harmless character smile, I leaned on the buzzer and waited. A man's voice shouted something inside, then there were heavy footsteps, the door opened, and there stood Michael Brooks, late of the Hotel Paradise.

It was even money which of us was the more surprised, but I had the edge. Brooks was in his shirt sleeves, and I quickly showed him the gun. There was real fear on his flabby face.

"How did you — ?"

"Never mind that," I snapped. "Inside."

"No. No wait." Despite the gun, he put out an imploring hand. "Look, don't get them mixed up in this. I'm begging you. I'll come out."

A woman's voice came from upstairs. "Who is it, Mickey?"

"Friend of mine," he called, sweat beads thick on his forehead, and rolling down. "I have to go out. Something's come up. I'll see you later." Then to me, quietly, "I'll just go get my coat."

"Oh no," I decided. "you come just the way you are, and right now. That, or we go inside."

He swallowed, nodded, and came out. I stood well clear of him as he pulled the door shut. I let him walk ahead of me, between the well-tended shrubs, the automatic back in my pocket. To anyone who might be watching, we were just two men going for a ride.

"You drive."

I tossed him the keys, and climbed into the rear. Trembling pudgy fingers located the ignition, and he started the motor.

"Where are we going?" he demanded nervously.

"I haven't been out in the desert lately. Let's admire some scenery."

He didn't like it, even the back of his neck said that, but he managed to retain control of the wheel, and soon we were clear of the last houses, and heading out towards Six. Another two miles, and there was just a dirt road off left. Tapping his shoulder with the gun, I motioned him to make the turn. As soon as we were out of sight of the highway, I made him pull off the road and stop.

"Out," I ordered.

He didn't want to get out. He knew too much about what happens to guys who drive out in the desert, and only one of them has a gun.

"You gonna kill me?" he demanded hoarsely.

"That's up to you," I replied dispassionately. "Out."

With the greatest reluctance, he rolled out of the driving seat. I was already out, and ten feet away, pointing the gun at his middle.

"Throw me the keys," I commanded.

He heaved them across, and I slipped them in my pocket.

"We'll take a walk, you first."

The heavy legs stumbled unwillingly over the hard-packed sand. A giant cactus was throwing a fair strip of shade, and I decided we had gone far enough. Planting myself in the shade, I ordered him to stop.

"Sit down."

I lit a cigaret, and watched as he squatted miserably in the full glare of the sun.

"Let's understand each other, Michael," I began. "I'm going to take you back into town, after we've had our little talk. You'll either be alive or dead, and I don't personally give a damn one way or the other. Like I said before, it's up to you. Start talking."

"Listen," he implored, "I don't know what — "

"Yes, you do," I interrupted. "Start with Griswold. Why'd you have to kill him?"

"I didn't mean to," he burst out, "the stupid bastard — that is — who says I killed him?"

"I do, for one, but that isn't important. The lady in the next apartment got a good look at you. She'll make a positive on you."

"That don't scare me," he bluffed. "One crazy dame. What kind of a witness is that? Any lawyer — "

"Now, now, Michael, you're forgetting something. We're not talking about lawyers, and courtrooms. The lady will probably be going to the morgue to see you. The lawyer hasn't been born who could get you off the slab. Like I said, it's up to you."

The desert stillness was all around. I clicked the safety on and off a couple of times. It sounded like the crack of doom. Brooks began to shake.

"What do you want to know?" he demanded, querulously.

"All of it," I replied. "But first tell me this. After you bumped off Griswold, where did you put those stones?"

"I didn't find 'em," he shouted, "Christ, do you think I'd be sitting around that crummy house if I had the stuff? I'd have been long gone, you can believe that."

Trouble was, I was inclined to.

"Start at the beginning," I instructed. "You and Griswold had this plan. You knew all about Walter Keane's movements, because he always let your sister go home to take care of mother, whenever he was away. But you couldn't dream up a scheme like this at a couple of day's notice. You must have planned it way back, and then waited for your chance. Right?"

He made no answer, but stared at the ground. The gun sounded like a bazooka on the still air, and a puff of sand flew up close to his fat legs.

"For Chrisakes," he yelled.

"An accident," I assured him. "My hand jumps around like that sometimes. The only thing that seems to calm it down, is the sound of a human voice. Talk to me, Michael."

He had to make several convulsive swallows before he got his vocal cords in any shape to speak.

"All right, all right. Just don't kill me, O.K? I'll tell you anything, everything, but just don't kill me."

"No promises," said nastily. "So start."

"You're right about the idea," he admitted. "We put it together weeks ago. I would always know when Keane was going to make a trip, like you said, because of Betty. She don't mean no harm, but she just loves to talk about her job. Coupla questions is all I need as a rule. The thing was, we had to pick a time of day when Jack was on shift. We almost pulled the stunt three weeks ago, but Keane was leaving at eleven thirty. Jack was on the midnight to eight, and it wouldn't have looked good, for him to volunteer for extra duty. Besides, there wasn't much chance of smog at that hour of the morning. We needed that smog."

I didn't understand that part. Smog, unless it's unusually severe, does not involve the abandonment of aircraft. It simply means that people have to sit and wait it out.

"Are you lying to me?" I demanded sharply, pointing the Colt.

"No, I swear to God," he trembled. "Why?"

"Smog doesn't bring out the Emergency crews," I spat, "so what made it important? And don't tell me you were waiting until some maniacs planted a bomb, because I don't think I can control my hand, if you do. And don't tell me those terrorists were working for you."

Some of the panic went from his face, to be replaced by astonishment, which, under the circumstances, I had to believe was genuine.

"You still haven't figured this out, have you? You haven't figured it no way at all."

"I don't have to," I reminded, tapping at the gun. "I have you, and I have this. You figure it for me. Oh dear, I can feel my hand shaking."

"Wait," he shouted, "wait. All right, all right. There ain't no terrorists. We made up the whole thing. The whole damn thing. It was beautiful."

"You didn't make up the bomb," I pointed out. "That was real."

"Sure it was. That's why we needed the smog. Jack makes the call, there's a payphone just outside emergency, then goes back in to wait for the balloon. He has the bomb with him, all set-up. When they get out there, you can just imagine what's going on. All he has to do is walk under the plane, tape the thing anywhere, and get back to work."

"Risky," I pointed out. "Suppose somebody saw him?"

"No sweat," he explained. "If anybody sees him, he yells that he's found the bomb. He's a hero, that's what he is. It means we gotta think again, but nobody goes to jail. They'd probably give him a medal or something."

Amazing to think that such a neat and adaptable scheme could be cooked up by this trembling jelly of a man and one other. I'd been too quick in dismissing Michael Brooks the previous day. Well, I wasn't going to make the same mistake twice. Trouble was, what was my next move? I had Griswold's killer, I had the explanation for the phoney terrorists, and all round, a lot of people were going to be very pleased with me. Everybody, that is, except the man who was paying the check. J. J. Fontaine had brought me into this for one reason only, and that had been to find his diamonds. That I hadn't done, and the rest of the kudos was very nice, but you couldn't cash it.

"So, in the end, everything worked

out," I mused unnecessarily. "Jack. got away with the goods, and the next day you killed him. Talk to me about that, Michael. Why'd you rub out your partner?"

He hesitated, then looked at the Colt and upwards into my unfriendly face. With a man in such a bad physical shape, my only worry was that he might decide to have a stroke or something. Not that I cared what happened to him, but a thing like that could make him a real dead weight to my progress.

"I'm waiting," I reminded nastily.

"Wasn't my fault," he muttered stubbornly. "We had a scheme, it was all agreed. Jack wanted to change things. Said he took all the risks, he ought to get the thick end. Fifty fifty was the deal, right from the gun. Now, he wants seventy five. I wasn't about to sit still for a shakedown like that, not after all the work I put into this thing. Plus, without me, there wasn't nothing. I was the one who knew Keane's movements. I had this gun, and I waved it at him. I wanted my half then and there. He tells me he hasn't got it. He's hid it somewhere, in case I turned nasty. Figured it might happen, he said. I didn't believe him, I start turning the place over. Jack gets sore and starts a ruckus, and next thing I know, the gun's going off all over the place, and here's old Jack, all dead on the floor. I tell you, it turned my stomach."

"I can imagine. What'd you do then?"

The fat frame shook.

"Guess I lost my head. I looked around some more, then got out of there before the law turned up. Somebody coulda heard those shots I fired."

"Somebody did," I pressed while it hurt, "the same lady who saw you leave. The one who's going to send you on that long walk."

An idea was beginning to form in my mind but it was still shadowy, and in need of blocking out. This jellyfish could help with that, if I could get any truth out of him.

"And that's all you know?" I queried. "You've no suggestion as to where Griswold could have tucked those stones? How about his brother's place, his cousin's?"

"Nah," he negatived. "Jack ain't got no family, nothing like that. No friends, either. Not real friends, people you'd trust with that kind of merchandise. It beats me."

"You looked in the obvious place?" I insisted, "his medical kit?"

He looked affronted, scared as he was.

"You gotta be out to lunch," he protested. "First place I looked. I tore that thing apart, new as it was. There was nothing, just his medicine junk. Listen you gotta believe me, the jam I'm in right now, if I had them rocks I'd give 'em to you, all of 'em, if I just get off this murder rap."

He meant it, at the moment. But I've seen people under stress before. They'll promise you anything, when the heat's on. Later, when you show up with the check, they develop memory lapses.

"Suppose I could come up with something?" I offered casually. "Something that might make them go easy on you? Say a small rap, two to five maybe, plus a few bucks in your pocket when you come out. How would you take to a proposition like that?"

"Like a duck to water," he said fervently. "Ah, but you're only kidding me. You ain't got nothing to play with."

"Consider the alternative," I suggested. "I scrag you right now, dump you in the car and take you back a dead terrorist and a new hero. Me. I'll be the one who gets the medal. Always wanted a medal. How'd you like them apples?"

"I don't, I really don't. Whaddya wanna kill me for? What good would it do? I'm nothing to you. I'm nothing to anybody."

"Except your own family," I corrected.

"Listen, you keep my family out of

275

this. They got no part in it. Things is bad enough for them without this dead terrorist talk. They're innocent people. Why do you want to drag them in?"

"They are in," I told him, without emotion. "The minute your name hits the papers and the tee vee, they'll be branded as members of the terrorist Brooks family. How much of that kind of hassle can they cope with? What'll they do when the first bricks come through the windows, Michael? When the shopkeepers won't serve them. When kids tear up the flowerbeds. People don't like terrorists, Michael. They get very nasty."

His eyes were killing me.

"You don't care who gets hurt, do you?"

"Just so I win," I stated calmly, "you want to listen to the proposition or not?"

"I said so, dinni," he grumbled sourly.

"First, the jewels are out. There never were any, there aren't going to be any. Nobody mentions them, nobody mentions them, nobody even thinks about them. Understand?"

His fat-rolled eyes were crafty now.

"What're you up to?"

"Hear me out. What happened was this. You'd heard Jack Griswold in the past talking crazy political stuff. He kept trying to get you involved in some wild scheme to blow up an airplane, show you meant business. You thought he was just talking wild, and used to calm him down. It's been going on for months. Are you getting all this?"

"I can hear what you're saying, but I don't get it," he admitted.

"Keep listening," I advised. "Now, all of a sudden you're mixed up in the bomb scare out at the airport, and you think about Jack right away. You see him there, when you come down the escape-chute, and you try to talk to him, but he just pushes you along, like all the other passengers. When the questions start, you're scared out of your wits. The people asking the questions think that's natural, seeing you just escaped with your life. But that's not what you're scared about, Michael. You're afraid because you think Jack might really have flipped his lid at last, but he's your buddy. You can't just hand him over unless you're sure. You keep stumm, because you're going to have this all out with Jack as soon as you're both clear of the airport. You're going to put it to him straight, and if he admits it, you're going to turn him in, buddy or no. You with me?"

"Then why didn't I?" he argued. "Why'd I kill him?"

"Accident. Just the way you described it. Only it wasn't your gun, it was his, and you managed to start a scuffle. The gun went off, and oh dear me, there's Jack on the floor, just as you said. Then you panic, and clear out. Before you go, you try to make it look like a burglary, like you were looking for valuables."

The heavy face was unhappy.

"I don't know. If I'm such a big citizen, killing this terrorist and all, why did I run away? Why didn't I go straight to the cops?"

"You're afraid to, at first. Anybody would be. You have to think, so you go to your sister's house. Then you send for me."

"Why would I do that?"

"Because I saw you at the Hotel Paradise," I explained patiently. "I said there might be a reward for information about the terrorists. You figured you were entitled to that, and besides I'm not a cop. You could talk to me, listen to me, get my advice."

Some kind of comprehension was now beginning to filter through. He nodded.

"You tell me I'm a hero, and your advice is to turn myself in. So where's this reward?"

"I have to talk to somebody about that," I hedged.

"O.K.," he made lumbering movements, as if getting up.

"Where d'you think you're going?" I demanded.

"Into town, ain't that right? Give myself up, like you said."

"Sit down, Michael. We have to go over this again. And again. You have to be word-perfect before we leave here. If I'm not satisfied, you leave feet first. Kabish?"

He nodded miserably. The sun was really getting to him now, and he'd probably lost ten pounds already. He could spare it.

"What do you think Griswold did with the diamonds?" I shot out.

But he really had been paying attention.

"What diamonds would those be?" he asked innocently.

"Now then, start off with Griswold. Where did you used to talk to him? When did it start?"

We stayed out there another hour. I moved every now and then to retain the scanty protection of the cactus, but Brooks was getting the full blast of the mid-day sun, and it was really bearing down on him by the time I was satisfied. It wasn't perfect, but what is? The homicide people would be happy because they had their killer. The security services would be more than happy to learn that their so-called terrorist organisation had a total membership of one, now deceased. There would be unexplained details, and I could expect a hard time from a number of sources, but that didn't bother me too much. A few people would yell, or mutter, according to fancy, but I'd lose no sleep. Overall, I hadn't done too bad a job, and the luck had run with me for once.

"Okay greaseball," and that just about described him, in the end. "On your feet. We're going to make a hero out of you."

He stumbled rather than walked towards the car. When we reached it, I told him to stop and turn round. The flabby face contorted with fear at the thought that I'd changed my mind, and was going to kill him after all.

"Just one final thing," I emphasised. "Just so you have the whole picture. You do this the way we rehearsed it, and it'll come out like I said. Do it wrong, and you're dead. Because if your story slips, you won't be any kind of hero at all. You'll be a heist artist who was willing to blow up an airplane and kill fifty innocent people just to get rich. Can you imagine what the law will do to you? There were women on that plane, kids. You know what goes on inside when the boys are alone. You think you can take that, Michael?"

He shuddered at the thought, and I knew he was going to make it. Now he put his hand on the door handle.

"You're not going in there," I informed him.

"Huh?"

I pointed to the rear.

"Luggage compartment for you. I can't take any chances on you changing your mind."

"It'll be two hundred plus in there," he screamed.

"You're too fat anyway. Get in."

I raised the lid, and heat flew out from the interior. It wasn't going to be a bundle of laughs for him, but I could take no risks at this late stage in the game. The last view I had was of his sweat-streaked face, where fear and hatred struggled for supremacy.

It was almost one-thirty when I pulled up outside the discreet private establishment where I hoped to find J. J. Fontaine. He'd evidently left word, and I was shown into a small cool ante-room to wait. Nobody had any right to look so cool and urbane in that heat, but then, he hadn't done my recent stint out in the desert.

"What news Mr. Preston?"

"I'm going to have to make this very quick, Mr. Fontaine. There's a man locked in the luggage compartment of my car and I don't know how long he can last in this heat."

He thought quickly, decided against questions.

"Then you want something from me. What is it?"

"I told you earlier that the murdered man Griswold probably stole your property," I reminded. "I now know it. The man locked in my car was his partner. No, he hasn't got your stuff, either. As I understand it, Griswold had no family, certainly no one around here. In other words, nobody will be claiming his property right away. There'll be a cousin or an uncle someplace, there always is, but it'll be a little while before he shows. Meantime, there's the question of Griswold's belongings out at the airport. There'll be a locker with some of his stuff in it, and there's a medical hand-kit. I've seen it, and it's brand new, so it must be worth several hundred dollars. Not something to leave unclaimed. The point is this, can you think up some legal fiddle-faddle? What we need is a lawyer to get out there with a power of attorney which allows him to take Griswold's property into custody, on behalf of the surviving relatives. Can it be done?"

He considered quietly, then inclined his head.

"Yes. I can arrange that. But don't you think your friends in Homicide will already have anticipated us?"

"Possibly. But the airport is outside the city's jurisdiction. It's county business, and those people don't exactly burst blood-vessels when it comes to co-operating with the city police. There are politics involved, and also certain personality clashes. If we're lively, that stuff will be in the hands of the Chief Security Officer, and he won't budge without proper legal clearance. I know him, his name is Filby, and he goes by the book. Have your man take the Griswold stuff out to your home, and I'll call you later."

"I will arrange it. And, by the way, your expert gave me a clearance on the telephone situation. The bug, as you call it, must be at your end only."

"Well, it's always best to check. I have a meeting with the F.B.I., at three o'clock. If they don't lock me up, I'll try to call you around four to four-thirty."

I rose to go, and he held out his hand.

"If anyone should do anything so hasty as to lock you up, Mr. Preston, I think you may have my assurance that the incarceration will be short-lived."

So he wasn't going to dump me. With people in his position you can never be sure. I put real feeling into the handshake before I left. There was a clump of trees at the side of the building, and I backed the car carefully towards them, braking when I was almost hidden from view. The I climbed out, and opened the rear lid. Brooks was a pitiful sight, a great mound of melting fat, with despair and misery written large on his face. He didn't attempt to get out, but huddled there, waiting.

"Let's go Michael. From now on,

you ride with me."

He rolled out, hands recoiling from the touch of hot metal.

"Where are we?" he wanted to know.

"Just ten minutes from the city center. We're going to my office now, and wait for some people. Police people. We'll have a clear hour to go through our story again. And again."

He was in no shape to argue or even talk very much. I had to give him some physical assistance before he was wedged into the front passenger seat. Michael Brooks was all through arguing about anything. I got him up to the office by the rear stairs, and lurched thankfully through the familiar door.

"My God."

Candy Sullivan was on her feet at once, and staring at the pair of us.

"Hi," I greeted. "This is Michael Brooks. He is in urgent need of some cold beer and sandwiches. Him and me both."

"You look like a couple of earthquake

victims," she pronounced. "What happened?"

That cactus tree had protected me from the worst of the sun, and I hadn't been riding in luggage compartments. All the same, I wasn't what you might call bandbox fresh, and it evidently showed.

"Nothing some grub won't put right," I assured her. "But, before you go, get Homicide for me please. Man's name is Randall."

To do her credit, she made no fuss, but just got on with it. By the time I had Brooks sprawled in a chair, the phone was ringing. Randall's pleasure at hearing my voice was well-concealed.

"This had better be good," he threatened. "We're very busy here."

"Try this," I suggested. "If you will come to my office at three o'clock, I think you will find I have the man who killed Griswold."

"The devil you say? Three o'clock. I'll be there, and you had better come good."

There's nothing to beat a little old-fashioned gratitude, I always say.

Candy was soon back with the restoratives, and Brooks pulled himself together sufficiently to tackle the food. I hoped my approach was a little more polished, but the intention was equally positive.

Candy grinned.

"Now will you tell me what happened?" she asked.

"Take too long," I refused. "Let me tell you what's going to happen. At three o'clock I'm holding a grand reception. Chief guests will be Agent Witchley of the F.B.I., and Sergeant Randall of Homicide. Neither of them knows about the other. Not yet. It would only lead to arguments about prior interests and whatever. They can have those here. Now then, at four o'clock — "

I paused, and looked at the chewing Brooks. Then I got up from my chair, took Candy by the arm, and lead her to the door, keeping my voice low. I told her what I wanted her to do at four o'clock, slipped off my jacket and handed it to her. The thirty eight felt heavy in the pocket. "Hang this up somewhere in your office, will you?"

She took it, nodding.

"These visitors," she asked hesitantly. "Are you going to be alright? You're not in any trouble are you?"

"Probably," I admitted. "They won't love me, that's for sure. But not real trouble, I don' think. Those people will trade Brooks for me any day. Don't forget our four o'clock call."

"I won't," she promised. "And you'll be careful?"

The concern on her face did my morale no harm at all.

"I'll be careful," I promised, turning back into the office. "Now then, Michael, let's go over it just one more time."

Brooks groaned.

9

ONE thing was certain. Both my visitors would arrive before time. It is rule number one of the streets, that you never stick to a time laid down by the opposition. You always get there early, to watch out for traps. Both Witchley and Randall were a long way from their street days, but early habits of that kind tend to stay with a man.

It was not much after two forty-five when Candy opened the door and announced formally.

"Mr. Witchley."

I tried to look annoyed, staring at my watch.

"Thought we said three o'clock?" I greeted.

"Did we?" he nodded carelessly. "Well, I was in the neigborhood anyway. Who's your visitor?"

"This is Michael Brooks, and he will have something important to tell you in a few minutes. Have a seat, Mr. Witchley."

He sat grudgingly down, staring at the man next to me.

"How do you mean, in a few minutes?" he demanded. "Listen, Preston, I don't have time for games — "

The opening of the door stopped him in mid-flow. Candy fluted, "Sergeant Randall."

Randall took one step inside, glowering around at the assembled company. Then he stuck out a hand to the F.B.I. man.

"We've met," he reminded. "Witchley isn't it? I'm Randall, Detective Sergeant, Homicide."

"How are you, Randall?"

Gil now looked at Brooks.

"This is the guy?"

"The very same," I confirmed. "Won't you sit down, Gil. There's a lot of explaining to be done."

"You can whistle that in F sharp

major," agreed Witchley, "and it had all better be very good indeed."

"Michael Brooks would like you gentlemen to hear what he has to say. I don't think you'll be bored. Go ahead, Michael, just the way you told it to me."

Brooks nodded. He didn't care any more. Physically and mentally he was beaten into the ground, and I was relying on his well developed instinct for self-preservation to triumph over his exhaustion. If he contrived to stick to the storyline we had hammered out, it would all turn out well. If he faltered or tripped, he was facing a minimum of twenty years, with a good lawyer, and I was facing — . No, I wouldn't even think about the possibility.

Haltingly, he began to tell the tale. In a strange way, I believe his obvious fear and insecurity told in his favour. When you looked at it from the point of view of a new listener, he was after all, confessing to the shooting of Jack Griswold, and that was a punishable crime, whatever his motives. And there was no doubt that he had their attention. Whenever his voice dropped, as it did occasionally, they leaned forward in their chairs, anxious to miss nothing. Lesser men would have interrupted him on points of clarification, but these were top operators. With a witness in the condition Brooks was in, a few sharp questions could throw him into a state of confusion, might cause him to withdraw altogether. They were both well aware of that, and were content to let him stumble along to the end. There would be time then for questions. When he finally reached the end, there was a heavy silence while they thought it through.

The first question came from Randall, and it surprised me.

"How'd you get in that condition, Brooks?"

"Condition?" The worried suspect looked at me, fearing a trap.

"Yeah, that's what I said," growled

Randall. "Look at the state you're in. Like somebody's been beating you up in a cellar for two days. That what you've been doing, Preston, beating it out of him?"

I looked affronted, impressing nobody.

"When Mr. Brooks told me his tale, I knew I was on to something big. But I didn't know him. Anybody can make up a yarn for reward money. I couldn't call you people right off not until I was certain. If we stayed around town, either of you gentlemen might have wanted one or other or us for some reason. So, we took a ride. We went out into the desert, where it's quiet. No interruptions. I tried every way I know to shake Mr. Brooks on his story, but I couldn't do it. I'm satisfied he's telling the whole truth. And that's why you're all here."

"You didn't threaten him, beat him up?" demanded Witchley. "Force him to say all these things?"

"Certainly not — " I began, but there was a yowl of protest from Brooks.

"That's a damned lie," he chattered, not daring to look at me. "He made me sit in the open desert while he sat in the shade with a gun, that's what he did. I could have fried to death for all he cared."

The two lawmen exchanged glances. It was Witchley's turn.

"So all this stuff was obtained under duress," he said softly. "That makes it worthless."

I could have strangled Brooks on the spot, not realising the cunning little animal was begining to take a real hand in the game.

"I was just using the gun as a fan," I explained.

"That's another lie," chimed Brooks. "He told me if I didn't tell him the whole truth, he'd blow holes in me. What he said was, if he turned me over to you guys and my story went bad, he stood to lose his license. I'll tell you he scared the hell out of me. I told him the truth alright. Who wouldn't?"

Some of the tension eased on the

other side of the table.

"Mr. Brooks," said Randall, and the 'Mr' was an innovation. "Agent Witchley and I are here now. You don't have to be afraid of this man any more. He knows better than to pull any stuff while we're around. If you want to change your story, any way at all, now's your chance. Do you?"

"What for? It's all true. Every word. Just like I told it to you."

"But you said Preston threatened you with a gun," Witchley pointed out. "Why did you bother to mention it?"

Brooks pouted.

"I don't see why he should get away with it, that's why. I come to him in all good faith to tell my story. Next thing I'm doing the oven thing in the middle of the desert with him threatening to blow my head off. He can't get away with treating me like that. Ain't there some kind of law? Could I sue him?"

Witchley looked sour.

"Anybody can sue anybody Mr. Brooks, but I think you're going to be too busy for the next few years for that kind of action. The first thing we have to have from you, and in a lot more detail, is a full statement about your claim that Griswold invented the Oppressed Peoples of America out of his head. That's a very important statement,and we are going to need chapter and verse on that. And that's just the begining. After we get through with you, you still have to convince Sergeant Randall with this yarn about how you killed Griswold in self-defense — "

"Just a minute," Randall held up a side-of-beef arm, and we were about to get the part I had anticipated. "I appreciate the Government's keen interest in this case, and believe me, every facility will be extended to your men. But this man has confessed to a homicide right here in this city, and that gives me the jurisdiction. I'm taking him in."

"You're taking him in?" whispered Witchley in disbelief. "I think I'm going to have to remind you of one or two points, sergeant. This is a Federal matter, a case for the Major Case Squad, of which I happen to be a member. The law — "

" — I know the law," snapped Randall. "This has been tested out before, and wound up at the Supreme Court — "

He clucked with annoyance and stopped talking as Candy Sullivan came into the room. It was exactly four o'clock.

"Sorry to interrupt Mr. Preston, but I need your signature if I'm to catch the post."

I grinned apologetically at my visitors. "Sorry gents, work must go on. I'll go outside and do it."

They got back to their squabble, and I closed the door behind me.

"Nice work, Candy. One or other of those guys is going to insist on taking me in as a material witness, and I have no intention of spending the weekend under those lights. Look,

I'm not coming back here. What time will you get home?"

"Five-thirty, thereabouts. Why?"

"I'll call you," I promised. "Can't just let you go disappearing out of my life this way."

She smiled, and not her office smile. "I was wondering about that."

Grabbing up my jacket, I opened the outer door softly.

"When they start to get angry, just remind them you're only from the agency. All you know is, I said I might not get back tonight."

"I will lock up promptly at five," she promised. "I'm expecting a call at home."

I hurried to the car and went straight to Parkside. There, I took a shower, found some fresh clothes, and tossed a few things in a bag. Then I locked up, and headed for the Fontaine house, stopping at a drugstore on the way to confirm I was on my way. When I arrived, Myrtle showed me straight in. Fontaine was alone in the room.

"You look remarkably fresh for a man who's been so busy," he greeted.

"You should have seen me an hour ago," I replied. "I looked like something the dog wouldn't eat. Did your man get the Griswold property?"

He nodded.

"It's on that table in the corner. Not very exciting I'm afraid. And you were right about Chief Filby. He read every word on that affidavit before he would release the stuff. What did you want it for?"

I was taking a gamble, and I knew it. Well, we'd soon know.

"You see this medical kit?" I hefted it across and laid it in front of him. "It's brand new. Griswold bought it the day of the bomb-scare, and bored the pants off the whole crew, showing off with it. That's Point One. Point Two is that these medics regard each other's kit as sacrosanct. That was the actual word used when they spoke to me. They would no more dream of touching a kit belonging to someone else, than you or I would of going through each other's pockets. They were quite touchy on the subject."

"I see. Go on."

"Point Three is that I third-degreed the man who killed him, name of Brooks. Brooks knew Griswold had the stones somewhere, and he turned the apartment over to find them. He ripped open the medical kit, threw the contents all over the floor. He was quite specific about it, and he had no reason to lie."

The smooth face threatened to wrinkle for a moment.

"An emergency bag perhaps?" he ventured.

"I hope not, Mr. Fontaine, I sincerely hope not. The way I map it out is like this. Griswold bought two new bags, not one. One was full of kit, the other empty. When he got to work that day, he stuck the empty one in the ambulance, so it was quite safe. After he got out to the plane, he was carrying his new kit, having first made certain everybody would know it. When Walter Keane was first jostled by Brooks, and then injected by Griswold, Griswold grabbed Keane's flat briefcase. He had to help him away from the chute. The other medics were busy with Passenger Howe and his blood problems. All Griswold had to do was to leave his medical kit on the ground, open up the second case, and slip Keane's bag inside, then tuck the whole thing out of sight. Under the stretcher, anywhere. When it was time to get clear he hopped into the ambulance, carrying the proper bag. The ambulance returned to the unit, and when Griswold jumped off he'd swapped bags. The medical kit was now under the stretcher, and the bag in his hand was the fake. He dropped it in the unit, in full view of everyone. Then the questions started, and they began a long night session before they could go home. Griswold was so tired he even forgot to take his bag with him, and no one was surprised. He would know it would be perfectly safe until he next came on duty, because that's the way those guys operate. Outside, he collects the first bag from the ambulance and carries it home. The plan was to do the same switching around the next time he came on duty. All the fuss would have died away by then, and nobody would be watching. Unfortunately for him, he decided to get greedy about the split, and Brooks killed him."

Two pairs of eyes were now staring at the bag.

"So if you're reasoning is correct, Walter Keane's little cargo is inside there?"

"I'm going to feel very foolish if it isn't," I admitted. "We'll have to force it. Griswold would have kept the key in his pocket."

"My privilege, I fancy," breathed Fontaine. He took a heavy paper-knife and inserted it behind the latch. One good heave and it flew open. He looked up at me and took a deep breath before lifting the lid. No bandages, no syringes, just a flat leather briefcase lay inside. The lawyer lifted it out, almost with reverence and produced a small gold key, which he turned in the lock, before unzipping the case. The desk seemed to catch fire as the afternoon sun struck at the heap of precious stones which spilled out. We both stared down, entranced. My heart was beating faster than normal.

It was Fontaine who recovered his composure first.

"You would seem to have recovered my property, Mr. Preston."

"I'm very relieved to hear it," I assured him thankfully. "That just leaves the question of Brooks defense. His deal with me is that no reference is made at any time to the diamonds. His killing of Griswold was a mixture of patriotic outrage and personal vengeance because he could have been killed. That's the way he'll tell it."

"And your deal with him?"

"So long as he sticks to the tale, and doesn't deviate, I have guaranteed him a top-level defense lawyer. I thought you would have no objection to arranging that?"

"You thought correctly. Mr. Brooks is a very lucky man, and if he sticks to the rules, he'll come out of this very well. Tell me Mr. Preston, what is your position in all this vis-a-vis the police and other authorities?"

"Not too bad, on the whole. They'll haul me in, get statements from me, generally give me a going over, but nothing I can't handle. But they're going to have to wait until Monday. I'm not going to spend the weekend trudging in and out of police stations. I'm off."

"Off where?"

"Damned if I know," I admitted. "I'll just drive out to the airport, pick the first flight that's heading for palm trees and silver beaches, and just climb aboard."

He managed to take his eyes off the diamonds at last, and slipped his hand inside a drawer.

"Then this should prove useful."

'This' was a bulky manila envelope, stuffed with fifties and hundreds, all used bills.

"It's all there," he assured me. "Twelve thousand five hundred, as we agreed originally. Together with my personal thanks. You have saved a number of people from embarrassment Mr. Preston, and I shall ensure they are all well aware of it."

"Thank you."

I meant it. You can't buy publicity like that. We shook hands, and I told the waiting Myrtle goodbye. Then I drove to a quiet bar, ordered a beer and pulled a telephone into reach.

Candy Sullivan answered at once.

"It's that man," I announced.

"I was hoping it would be. I'm afraid your visitors weren't very pleased with you."

"Could we talk about it later? Over dinner? I know a great place, right on the beach, where you can watch the fishing boats."

"Is it far?" she queried.

"Ensenada," I replied, and waited.

"That's in Baja California isn't it?"

"Right," I confirmed. "If we take the seven o'clock plane, we'll be eating by ten. We can eat, swim, laze around, whatever you want. What do you say?"

"What would the arrangements be?" She meant the sleeping arrangements.

"You can choose when we get there," I promised. "No pressure."

"You mean that?"

"I mean it."

"Then I'd better hurry. Seven o'clock flight. You don't give a girl much room to manoeuver. Lordy, I shall have to come more or less as I am."

"Just so as you come. Gate Three at six forty-five. I'll have the tickets."

"Mark," she interjected. "When are we coming back?"

"Same answer, it's up to you. But I'm hoping you won't want to hurry."

"So'm I."

With which enigmatic reply, she hung

up. I was still wondering what she meant as we boarded the plane.

Well, a man can only hope.

THE END

A GENTEEL LITTLE MURDER
Philip Daniels

Gilbert had a long-cherished plan to murder his wife. When the polished Edward entered the scene Gilbert's attitude was suddenly changed.

DEATH AT THE WEDDING
Madelaine Duke

Dr. Norah North's search for a killer takes her from a wedding to a private hospital.

MURDER FIRST CLASS
Ron Ellis

Will Detective Chief Inspector Glass find the Post Office robbers before the Executioner gets to them?

A FOOT IN THE GRAVE
Bruce Marshall

About to be imprisoned and tortured in Buenos Aires, John Smith escapes, only to become involved in an aeroplane hijacking.

DEAD TROUBLE
Martin Carroll

Trespassing brought Jennifer Denning more than she bargained for. She was totally unprepared for the violence which was to lie in her path.

HOURS TO KILL
Ursula Curtiss

Margaret went to New Mexico to look after her sick sister's rented house and felt a sharp edge of fear when the absent landlady arrived.

THE DEATH OF ABBE DIDIER
Richard Grayson

Inspector Gautier of the Sûreté investigates three crimes which are strangely connected.

NIGHTMARE TIME
Hugh Pentecost

Have the missing major and his wife met with foul play somewhere in the Beaumont Hotel, or is their disappearance a carefully planned step in an act of treason?

BLOOD WILL OUT
Margaret Carr

Why was the manor house so oddly familiar to Elinor Howard? Who would have guessed that a Sunday School outing could lead to murder?

THE DRACULA MURDERS
Philip Daniels

The Horror Ball was interrupted by a spectral figure who warned the merrymakers they were tampering with the unknown.

THE LADIES
OF LAMBTON GREEN
Liza Shepherd

Why did murdered Robin Colquhoun's picture pose such a threat to the ladies of Lambton Green?

CARNABY
AND THE GAOLBREAKERS
Peter N. Walker

Detective Sergeant James Aloysius Carnaby-King is sent to prison as bait. When he joins in an escape he is thrown headfirst into a vicious murder hunt.

MUD IN HIS EYE
Gerald Hammond

The harbourmaster's body is found mangled beneath Major Smyle's yacht. What is the sinister significance of the illicit oysters?

THE SCAVENGERS
Bill Knox

Among the masses of struggling fish in the *Tecta*'s nets was a larger, darker, ominously motionless form . . . the body of a skin diver.

DEATH IN ARCADY
Stella Phillips

Detective Inspector Matthew Furnival works unofficially with the local police when a brutal murder takes place in a caravan camp.